I0691404

THE FOLKS ON TAYLOR CIRCLE

First Edition

Published by The Nazca Plains Corporation
Las Vegas, Nevada
2010

ISBN: 978-1-61098-001-2
E-book: 978-1-61098-002-9

Published by

The Nazca Plains Corporation ®
4640 Paradise Rd, Suite 141
Las Vegas NV 89109-8000

PUBLISHER'S NOTE
The Folks on Taylor Circle is a work of fiction created wholly by *Greg Bowden*'s imagination. All characters are fictional and any resemblance to any persons living or deceased is purely by accident. No portion of this book reflects any real person or events.

Cover Photo, Stella Levi
Cover Design, Ian Ray
Art Director, Blake Stephens

DEDICATION

For John who has seen me through three of these things now and says he's actually looking forward to the fourth. Greater love hath no man than this. Thank you, Sir.

And to Eagle Eye Paul who knows more about the English language than I ever will and is oh, so gentle with me about my errors. You are very much appreciated, Paul.

And, of course, for The Prime Timers of the Desert who always offer encouragement, fascinating examples and friendship. These guys are First Class.

THE FOLKS ON TAYLOR CIRCLE

First Edition

Greg Bowden

CONTENTS

PROLOGUE

Taylor Circle is perhaps the smallest cul-de-sac in Palm Springs, California. It contains exactly five homes and was developed between 1968 and 1971 by a contractor named John Clark, who built each of the five homes himself. He named the street Taylor Circle after a movie actress whom he always thought of as "My Raven-haired Goddess." Of course he couldn't tell that to his wife—who was a blond and rather small-bosomed—so he led her to believe that the street was named for Zachary Taylor, 12th President of the U. S. and an all-around swell guy.

The first house he built was Number Fifty, which is the first house you see when you drive into the circle, in the twelve o'clock position, as it were. That house sold before it was even finished and gave him the seed money for the next one, Number Twenty-Nine, which was next door, in the ten o'clock position. When that was sold, he went on to Number Fifteen (eight o'clock) which was followed by Numbers Seventy-Eight (two o'clock) and Ninety-Five (four o'clock).

All the homes have essentially the same floor plan, although there is some variation. For example, the folks who bought Number Twenty-Nine suggested that he should incorporate an outdoor shower into the master bath; something with a privacy screen around it, shielding it from the yard and pool area but open to the sun and the spring and fall breezes that make desert living so delightful. All the following homes got such a shower, and before the 1980's were finished the others had been retrofitted. John Clark was that sort of man.

The homes, though pretty similar inside with three bedrooms, two full bathrooms and a small powder room off the entry, were all quite distinctive and individual on the outside. Number Fifty, the first one, was rather plain with masonry walls painted "Desert Sand" and the usual glass block insert by the front door, giving the entry hall outdoor light. The pool was rectangular and a little too big for the back yard. The windows were also not as large as they should have been.

These design details were corrected as Mr. Clark built his way around the circle. Pools became freeform and smaller, and windows grew larger until, by Number Ninety-Five, the living room and master bedroom walls, those looking out on the back yard and pool, were mostly glass. The landscaping also got a lot more creative, starting with Number Fifteen when Mr. Clark caught the landscape contractor cheating on the price of palm trees and fired him.

The new man, who was gay by the way, although Mr. Clark hadn't a clue about that, and his partner thought up unique arrangements of plants and trees and generally minimized the water-sucking lawns everyone else in town was planting. By 1985 the lawns at Numbers Twenty-Nine and Fifty had been scrapped as well, in favor of small plots intended for the various dogs who were residents of the circle. As a little joke, the landscaper and his partner, both of whom had had some years of experience in the wooded section of Griffith Park in Los Angeles, put a miniature forest of palm trees, thick bushes and hidden nooks at Number Ninety-Five. No one actually figured out this little labyrinth until 2000 when a pair of gentlemen bought the house and soon saw the possibilities.

Over the years of course Taylor Circle changed its character. Where originally the homes had been occupied by younger families, by the 1990's the occupants were mostly older, retired folks whose children had grown and moved on in the world. The first of those older folks to leave were Sam and Doris Kleiner at Number Twenty-Nine.

It was mostly Doris' idea to move. She had grown tired of the heat of summer in the desert and longed for the company of her daughter and her grandchildren, who lived in Virginia. Sam liked the desert and the peace of small-town living but finally gave in when Doris told him that their son-in-law had bought a condo as an investment and was offering it to them, rent free, for as long as they wished to live there. He gave in for two reasons:

first, if he didn't, Doris would never stop talking about it, and second, in his heart, he really wanted to spend time with his grandchildren too. He figured the pleasure of the children would outweigh the pain in the ass that was his son-in-law.

Number Twenty-Nine Taylor Circle went on the market the 10th of May, 1998. It sold in seven days to a couple named Wesley Benson and William Davis, who took possession on June 1, 1998.

CHAPTER ONE

WES & BILL

Wes and Bill met in 1991 on the front walk of the Mountain View Elderly Care Home in Phoenix, Arizona. Wes was seventeen—though he'd tell you he was "almost eighteen" if you asked him his age—and working as a part-time gardener at the home. Bill was thirty-two.

Bill had rather reluctantly checked his mother into the Home the week before, after flu had left her too weak to care for herself. He had a feeling in the pit of his stomach that she would finally leave the Mountain View Elderly Care Home in a pine box, and the thought saddened him greatly. His mother, who had long ago earned the title "One Strong Lady," pooh-poohed the idea and said this was only a temporary stay until she could get back the strength she had lost in that bout with the flu.

Wes noticed Bill that very first day and made it his business to find out what he could about him. The front-office nurses, who all liked Wes greatly, were very helpful in that endeavor and received a box of chocolates for their efforts.

Mrs. Davis also received a present: a large mixed bouquet of flowers from the home's gardens. When Bill visited her the next day he asked her about them.

"Oh, my yes, aren't they pretty?" she said. "He said they would brighten up the room and they really do, don't they?"

Bill scratched his head. "He? Who is 'he'?"

"Oh, you know, that young friend of yours. I believe he's called Wes. Yes, I'm sure that's what he told me." She lay back against her pillow and her eyes seemed to want to close. "We had a nice conversation." Her voice faded off into a quiet snore.

Bill sat by her bed for a while, until a pretty nurse came in and told him his mother would probably sleep for a couple of hours. As she was leaving he asked the nurse if she knew someone by the name of Wes.

"Oh, yes," she smiled. "He's the high-school boy who mows the lawns and stuff." She thought for a moment. "Yes, I think he did come and visit with Mrs. Davis for a while yesterday. Brought her those flowers." She pointed at the bouquet.

Bill thought for a moment and decided that he should thank this kid who brought his mother flowers. "He still around?"

"Who? Oh, Wes. Yeah, I think I saw him putting the mower away." A bell rang and she consulted her watch. "That's old Mrs. Clark. A dear but a little difficult if she feels ignored for too long. See you later."

Bill made his way down the hall and out the front door. He spotted a good-looking young man watering some rather bedraggled flowers and went over to him.

"You," he pointed. "Wes?"

The boy looked up and smiled. "Yes sir, Mr. Davis." He stuck his hand out.

When they shook hands they both felt something pass between them. Bill had no idea what it was and simply nodded and dismissed it. Wes, on the other hand, nodded and grinned, as though he'd expected it.

"Thank you for the flowers. They made my mother very happy."

"I'm glad. Those rooms are pretty drab and need something to brighten them up."

There was a pause, but before it could become awkward, Wes filled it by saying, "You look like you could use a cup of coffee and maybe a cookie." He reached down and shut off the water. "Come on. That place across the street there has really good coffee. I'll buy." He pulled Bill to the sidewalk, linked arms with him and started walking.

"Well, uh… I don't know. I mean…" By the time he got all this out it was too late. They were crossing the street, heading for Gourmet Grocers. Wes indicated Bill was to sit at one of the tables in the little garden facing the street.

"Cream, sugar, what?" Wes asked.

"Oh, uh, black, please."

"Just like God made it. I thought so," Wes said cryptically and disappeared inside the store.

He came back carrying two mugs of coffee and a large sugar cookie in a fold of waxed paper. He set Bill's coffee in front of him, sat, and placed the cookie exactly between them. "They had some wonderful-looking chocolate chip ones but I didn't want to get too wild, at least not the first time." He raised his coffee cup. "Cheers."

Bill tasted his coffee and found it to be exceptional. "Uh, why the flowers? I mean, you don't know her, do you?"

Wes smiled. "I do now. Her name is Edna and she absolutely loves to talk about you."

Bill laughed. "I know she does, far too much. But you didn't answer my question: why flowers and why her?"

There was a small pause while Wes weighed his options. As always, honesty came out on top. "So I could meet you." He broke the cookie in two, pushed the larger part toward Bill and then took a bite out of the smaller.

"Me? Why me?"

"Well, first of all, you're hot." Wes, still holding the cookie, touched his index finger, ticking off his points. "You're kind, you're sensible, you think things through. Oh, and did I mention that you're hot?"

Bill kind of harrumphed his disapproval but knew he was blushing anyway. Nobody had ever called him hot before.

"Well, you are." Wes dipped his cookie in his coffee. "And your mom likes me."

"She likes anybody who doesn't talk back to her."

"You're worried about her, aren't you?"

Bill sighed. "Yes, I suppose I am." He shrugged. "They tell you all this stuff about modern care and super drugs but they really don't know anything, do they? Not about just one specific person."

Wes put his hand on Bill's arm. "But you do, don't you. You know what you know in your gut."

Bill gave him a thoughtful look. "Yeah, I do. But I don't want to." He finished his part of the cookie. "Look, I've got to go. Thank you for the coffee. Next time it's on me." He got up and left, crossing the street and turning toward the nursing home.

It took Wes several more minutes to sort out his feelings. On top, he was elated by Bill's "next time" statement. But under that he felt sorry for him and what he was going through. Below that was a fullness that he quickly recognized as an erection. The man, after all, was hot.

That evening, sitting in his easy chair and sipping a scotch and soda, Bill thought about the afternoon and wondered what might have been going through the mind of that boy, Wes. Then it came to him: the boy was coming on to him. "Well, I'll be damned," he said out loud. It wasn't often that someone as young and handsome as that boy came on to him. In fact, it was never, before that afternoon.

The next day Bill was determined to nip this thing—whatever this thing was—in the bud, but Wes frustrated him by not being there. On top of that, his mother kept talking about Wes and what a nice young man he was.

When he left, he asked one of the nurses about Wes, and she said he only worked Monday, Wednesday and Friday afternoons. "You know," she said, "he's a real ambitious boy. Works hard and I hear that he's very popular at school, especially with the girls." She told him how fond everybody was of Wes and what a kind boy he was, always bringing in candy or flowers for the nursing station. By the time Bill left he was convinced that no boy like Wes could be coming on to him. He must have been mistaken.

The next day, when Bill got to the home, Wes shut off his mower and came over to the sidewalk. "Hi, Mr. Davis. She's... well, she's not having a good day. I told her you'd be in to see her this afternoon and that seemed to help but... well, I'm not sure she knew exactly when 'this afternoon' might be." He put a hand on Bill's arm. "Give her a hug. She'll like that better than anything."

Bill nodded and thanked him. When he saw his mother, he saw what Wes had meant. She was pale and her eyes looked a little blank. She knew him, though, and tried her best to smile. "That sweet friend of yours came to see me this..." She looked away, at the wall. "Well, I don't know when it was but he cheered me up and brought those lovely flowers over there." She nodded at a vase of flowers and then looked up at him. "You're lucky to have a kind friend like him, dear. We all need kind friends like him."

He sat down and took her hand. "Yes, he's a good..." What? He shrugged. "A good boy."

When his visit was over, signaled by his mother's falling asleep, he went outside and stood on the porch watching Wes watering some new seedlings in the place where the dying flowers had been last time. When Wes saw him, he turned off the water, wiped his hands on his jeans and grinned.

"Ready for coffee? It's your turn to buy, remember."

So Bill bought the coffee and splurged on a large double-chocolate cookie.

Over the next three weeks Bill and Wes had coffee and a cookie every Monday, Wednesday and Friday after Bill's visit with his mother. It wasn't long before Bill truly looked forward to these meetings and not long after that that he became a bit dependent on them. Wes was always a good listener and always had cheerful things to say about something. And he always made sure that Bill's mother had fresh flowers in her room.

During those rare times when Bill actually thought about it, he knew something else was going on but he just couldn't bring himself to think about what it might be. He had essentially given up sex during this period too, but figured that was a function of being constantly worried about his mother.

And then, of course, the inevitable happened: his mother died. It was a quiet passing, in the middle of the night, the nurses said. She went with a small teddy bear tucked into the crook of her arm, a gift from Wes. It had, the nurses said, given her comfort.

Bill missed seeing Wes on Friday because he was tied up with funeral arrangements. He figured he wouldn't see him until Monday when he'd go to the nursing home and buy him one last coffee and cookie.

As usual where Wes was concerned, he was wrong.

On Saturday, during the funeral, Bill looked around and there he was, sitting in the back. He was dressed in dark gray trousers and a dark blue blazer, complete with a white shirt and gray tie. He had a white carnation in his buttonhole. Somehow Bill found his presence comforting.

Afterwards, while everybody was standing around giving Bill their condolences, Wes stepped up, hugged him and said, "I'll see you Monday afternoon." It was only after he had left that Bill realized the white carnation was now in his own buttonhole.

For Bill, Monday afternoon had an eerie quality to it. It seemed just like the past four or five Mondays, washing up, leaving work, driving to the nursing home; almost like nothing had changed. But of course it had and, in fact, he had no real reason, he thought, to see Wes at all.

Wes bought the coffee and came out with a sugar cookie in a fold of waxed paper, just like the first time. They talked about nothing much for a while, until Bill finally couldn't stand it.

"Wes, what's going on here? What are we doing?"

Wes smiled at him and took a sip of coffee. "Let's not talk about it today, okay? Maybe Wednesday or next week but not today. You're still pretty broken up about your mom and probably not thinking as well as you usually do."

"But Wes…"

"No. Maybe Wednesday."

And so any discussion of what might be happening was deferred until Wednesday.

On Wednesday Bill took the bull by the horns. "Look, we need to talk a little," he said after he'd gotten the coffee and cookie. "I've been thinking about this a lot and I remembered what you said, that first time. You said that you took my mother flowers so you could meet me. You also said that you find me…" He almost laughed but realized Wes was quite serious. "Hot. So again, what the hell is going on here?"

Wes sighed and sipped his coffee. "What's going on here," he said quietly, "is that we need to spend some time together."

"Why?"

There was a long silence while Wes put his coffee down, wiped his mouth with a napkin and looked off into space for a moment. "Because at some point you and I are going to spend the rest of our lives together so we might as well start getting used to each other now."

Bill's first impulse was to laugh. His second was to get up and run like hell. Fortunately he was able to suppress both. "And why would you say that?"

"Don't you remember? That first time we shook hands? I know you felt it; I saw it in your eyes."

Bill, to his credit, thought about it and remembered. To his even greater credit, he nodded. He had no idea what to say.

"I did too. So we need to make peace with it. And with each other."

They stared at each other while they finished their coffee in silence. When the coffee was gone Bill picked up the cups and napkins and threw them in the trash barrel. He sat back down, looked at Wes and said, "I don't know what to say or what to do. I think, therefore, that I will go home, have a drink and let my mind sort it all out."

Wes nodded. "Monday?"

"Yes, I think that will be enough time. You need a ride anywhere?"

Wes shook his head.

They went their separate ways.

Bill worked four hours overtime both Thursday and Friday on the theory that the longer he didn't think about Wes the easier it would be when he finally did. It wasn't. When he sat down Friday night to think about things, they were all a jumble of feelings, impressions and an odd fact or two. After a couple of hours he gave up and went to bed where he had every intention of masturbating. He couldn't even do that very well and finally gave up, turned onto his belly and went to sleep.

Saturday wasn't much better so he busied himself with cleaning and doing the laundry. All the while two phrases kept running around in his head: At some point we're going to spend the rest of our lives together. And: You're hot! What was that all about? An answer came to him while he was folding his underwear: Sex! That tall, handsome kid wanted to be with him so they could have sex! The boy was making a pass at him! He shook his head. That wasn't even credible. Even in his weirdest dreams nothing like that had ever happened. He decided to stop thinking.

After a light dinner he decided that maybe what he needed was companionship. Hot, sweaty, naked, male companionship. He even knew where to find it, or at least he thought he knew. A bar called Men. He'd seen it advertised in one of the gay throw-away papers. The ad had called it, "A place for Men to find Men who like to do what Men do with Men." He'd never been there—he hadn't been to many gay bars—but it had to be the place.

He changed into jeans and a white tee shirt. The only boots he had were ones he worked in so he had to settle for tennis shoes.

The bar was across town so it was late when he got there. It was crowded but he found a place at the bar between a young guy with more muscles than any man is entitled to have and a man his age wearing chaps, a leather jockstrap and no shirt.

He ordered a beer. Then another. Then a third. With the third beer he thought he'd better circulate, see who else was there. He finished his beer watching two guys play pool. Then he had to pee.

The men's room was pretty dark, with just enough light to see that it had a couple of sinks and a trough. There were four guys using the trough. Bill took the end spot, right next to the sinks. The man next to him was being played with by the next guy down. Then he realized that the guy standing at the sink on his other side was washing his dick instead of his hands. Bill took it all in and even managed to empty his bladder as well.

Just as he was finishing the man next to him moaned quietly and came into the trough. Bill tucked himself away and went out to order another beer.

Bill had six more beers that evening and went to the men's room four times, twice because he had to pee. Then, when he ordered another beer the bartender very kindly suggested that perhaps he needed home and bed more than another beer. To the bartender's surprise, Bill agreed with a minimum of cajoling. He balked a bit at the suggestion that he take a cab home but finally gave in when a cabdriver walked in and took him by the arm.

"Let's go, Buddy," he said. "Where to?"

Bill managed to give his address—the cabdriver had him repeat it twice—and the bartender wrote the word "car" and the bar address on a card and tucked it into Bill's pocket.

When they got to his house the cabdriver helped him up the steps and helped him open his front door. "You know, Buddy," he said, "you're going to get hurt someday, drinking like that. Too bad, too, because you are one hot man." He then kissed him on the mouth, made sure Bill went inside and locked the door behind him, and then left.

Bill got up three times that night getting rid of the beer.

In the morning he was puzzled by two things: why there weren't any tire marks where the truck had run over him and why were his dick and balls all sticky?

After three aspirins and a very long, very hot shower he decided that he hadn't actually been hit by a truck, he just felt that way. As to the sticky genitals, he just didn't want to know.

His clothes, even his shoes, all smelled of beer, cigarette smoke and, faintly, urine. Another thing he didn't want to know about. When he came across the card with the word "car" and the address on it he wished he'd tipped the bartender better.

He washed down more aspirin with a pint of orange juice, got dressed and went to find his car. The fresh, cool air really helped his recovery, to the point that he jogged the last mile and a half. The café next to the bar was open so he went in and had buttermilk waffles and coffee for breakfast before retrieving his car and going home.

The rest of the day was spent reading, napping and watching a game on TV, anything so he didn't have to think.

When he arrived at the nursing home on Monday he still didn't know what he was going to say to Wes.

At the market Bill sat at a table and said, "Hey, it's your turn. And how about getting one of those double-chocolate things, huh?"

Wes grinned and went in to get the coffee and cookie. When he brought them to the table he laughed. "First I worried that you wouldn't show up at all and then, when you did, I worried that you were going to tell me no way. Shows how dumb I am, huh?"

Bill tasted his coffee and found it as good as the very first time. "How do you know I'm not? Going to tell you 'no way,' I mean."

"Because if you were, you would have insisted on buying."

"You do pay attention, don't you?" He broke the cookie in two and pushed part over in front of Wes. "God, I like these things," he said, taking a small bite. "Rich, though. Very rich. Can't…"

"Bill? You're rambling."

Bill stopped and thought for a moment. "Yeah, I am. It's because I don't know what to say. I mean, about…"

Wes smiled and put a hand on his arm. "Us. You don't know what to say about us." He paused and sipped his coffee. "But that's okay. You've decided we can get to know each other better. That's enough, for now."

They sat in silence for a couple of minutes before Bill said, "There is one thing we do have to talk about now. Sex. At least, sex between us."

Wes suddenly turned wary. "What… why?"

Bill took a deep breath. He'd had no idea he was going to bring this up now, today. But here it was. "Because you are seventeen and I am thirty-two and there are rules about things like that."

Wes interrupted. "It's okay. I looked it up. After sixteen I'm okay."

"I have my own rules."

"I know you do. Or I should have known. But look at it from my point of view. I'm considered by my parents and my teachers as a fairly mature guy. They all think of me as a man. So does the state of Arizona. I can join the army, I can get drafted so I can kill people, I can even vote. Doesn't that…"

Bill sighed. "Yes, I suppose it does. If you can kill people I suppose you can make love to them as well." He took a long swallow of his coffee. "But you aren't there, yet."

Wes' eyes fell. "No…" He looked up, his eyes filled with determination. "Not yet but soon. And, if it really makes a difference to you, I can wait. I'll be eighteen in June. I can wait until then. After all," He held up his right hand, "Henry still has his best friend to help him out."

"Henry?"

Wes did more to endear himself to Bill than he could ever know: he blushed.

A light went on in Bill's head. "Oh."

Still blushing, Wes ducked his head. "I know it's adolescent. I was, well, young and lots of guys...."

Bill reached out and touched Wes' hand, Henry's best friend. "Don't be embarrassed. Lots of guys do that."

"Lots of guys... Like you?"

Bill thought for a moment. "Not really." He paused and shrugged: in for a penny, in for a dollar. "I mean, he's never had a name exactly, he's always just been he. Even when I was a little kid, before I even knew what he could do, he was 'he'. Does that make sense?"

Wes smiled. "Yeah, I suppose it does. Sort of." His eyes were suddenly mischievous. "With a capital H?"

Bill caught on immediately. "No, unlike God, he remains in the lower case. He'll be jealous that Henry has the capital H but he'll get used to it." He drank the rest of his coffee and said, offhandedly, "No one else knows that, you know. That I think of him as 'he.'"

"My dad knows about Henry. I mean that I call him that." He finished his coffee. "But only him. Well, and now you. I was about seven when I told him. He thought it was cute, said maybe he'd name his."

Bill was surprised. He never could have had a conversation like that with his father. "Did he?"

"I doubt it. I think he'd have told me if he had." He grinned. "Why don't you ask him?"

"I think I'll wait until I know him a little better. Or at all, for that matter. What's he going to think about this—whatever this is? Or your mom?"

"They'll like you so I guess they'll think it's okay. You'll like them, too, especially my dad, so..." He shrugged his shoulders. "We'll see, won't we?"

"I guess we should do that sometime soon, don't you think?"

Wes nodded. "Yeah, Saturday. Mom's making scaloppini; she wants to impress you."

"Wait a minute. Saturday? They know about me?"

Wes shrugged again. "Well, yes. I mean, if you're going to court a guy then you better make sure your family is on board with it." He snapped his fingers. "Oh yeah, and Edna, your mother? She thought it was good too."

Bill was momentarily stunned. "You told my mother you were courting me?"

"Sure," Wes said. "Well, maybe not in so many words but she knew, and she thought it was a good thing. She said you needed somebody to love and take care of you."

Bill buried his head in his hands. "How did I get myself into this thing?"

"Because you're a good man, full of love and caring. You'll see, we belong together."

Over the next few months it became more and more apparent that Wes was right: they belonged together.

The dinner with Wes' parents. Kate and Ken, turned out to be easy, friendly and delicious. Kate was one hell of a good cook and took delight in pleasing others with her skill. After a few Sunday dinners Bill began to wonder how Wes and his father stayed so fit.

At first Bill was a little bothered by the fact that Wes and Ken talked about literally everything, but as time went on he saw the virtue of it. Wes trusted his father absolutely and Ken seemed never to be too busy or distracted to listen to Wes, no matter what the subject. At that first dinner Bill had expected to be taken aside by Ken and quizzed about his intentions—pretty much like any potential son-in-law would be. And that did happen except that he wasn't taken aside and Wes was included in the discussion.

A few weeks after that first dinner, Bill, Wes and Ken were sitting on the patio one afternoon, enjoying each other's company, when Ken said, "You know, I've been thinking about you guys and what you're doing, waiting until Wes is eighteen before you begin the physical side of your relationship. I'm really glad you're doing it that way and I'm rather proud of you both. I don't know though, I think it'd make me pretty cranky—not to say horny—if I had to do it."

Bill tried to imagine his own father saying something like that and couldn't do it. The only thing his father had ever said to him about sex was, "Wear a rubber!"

Ken looked at Bill and laughed. "Hey, I know this is maybe a little unconventional, but you know? If everyone talked to each other, there'd be a lot more happiness in the world. Anyway, what I was thinking was that you two guys should be careful with your masturbation fantasies."

Bill choked on his iced coffee. Wes jumped up and pounded him on the back. When Bill could breathe again, Wes said, "I guess you and your dad didn't talk about stuff like this, huh? See? I told you my dad was cool." He turned to Ken. "What about our fantasies?"

Ken chuckled. "Well, I don't know. But I've always talked to Wes about things so I guess you'd better get used to it, Bill. What I was thinking was that you guys should avoid fantasies involving each other. I guarantee that when you get down to actually doing it, it won't be anything like your fantasies. It never is and you don't want your first times to be marred by any silly expectations you've built up." He shrugged. "I just thought I'd throw that out for whatever it's worth."

It was worth a lot and both of them, after some discussion, decided it was a good thing.

A month or so later, sitting on Bill's couch one evening, Wes turned to him and asked, "What do you like to do? In bed, I mean."

Bill had known this was going to come up and had thought about it but still didn't know how to answer it. "I guess I'm pretty vanilla." At Wes' quizzical look he added, "I mean, I'm not into anything very extreme."

Wes chuckled. "I was pretty sure of that. No whips and chains, things like that?"

Bill shook his head. "No, no whips and chains. How about you? What are you into?"

Wes thought for a moment. "Well, I haven't done much of anything. Haven't had the opportunity I guess. But I know I'm going to like it—all of it. Even if it hurts at first." There was a long silence. Finally: "Do you like to do that?"

Bill sighed. He found it hard to talk about this stuff—sex—even with a man he was falling in love with. That thought made him sit up. It was the first time he'd allowed himself to think about that, that he was falling in love with Wes.

Wes, who was very perceptive where Bill was concerned, realized something was going on so he just took Bill's hand in his and let him have whatever time he needed.

Bill, for his part, pushed the thought into a little compartment in his head where he could take it out and examine it later, when he was alone. "Yeah, I like that. Both ways." He really pushed himself. "I like to suck cock, too."

Wes looked at him and grinned. He saw this as a major breakthrough. "Good. We'll get along just fine, I think."

On the first Wednesday in May, Wes was sitting on Bill's front balcony when Bill came home. "It happened," he said, kissing Bill and then handing him a sheet of paper. He was so excited that Bill was afraid he was going to float up into the air like a kid's circus balloon. The paper was a letter of acceptance from Stanford University.

"Oh, man, you did it!" Bill pulled him into a hug and whispered in his ear. "You were so afraid you wouldn't get in but we all knew you would. You're going to make us—and Stanford University—very proud."

Later, sitting with a beer which Wes had recently developed a taste for, Bill asked what his mother and father thought about it.

"They don't know yet. I got the mail and came over here. I was going to wait until you got home to open it, in case I got suicidal or something, but couldn't stand the suspense so I opened it anyway." He kissed Bill again.

"Well then, we'd better go and tell them."

"Yeah. Dad is going to be so happy. Especially since he won't have to pay for it."

"Of course he won't. I will."

That stopped Wes in his tracks. "Huh?"

Bill smiled. "Look, Wes, you once said we were going to spend the rest of our lives together. I understood that to mean that we were going to be Life Partners. Did I miss something?"

Wes shook his head.

"Then we, you and I, are a family, separate from the family who brought you up. You are my responsibility now, or will be on your eighteenth birthday, just as I am yours. You need an education and we, you and I, are going to see that you get it."

Wes stared at him for a long moment and then stepped so close to Bill that their bodies were touching from their knees to their chests. "Bill," he whispered, "I love you."

Bill leaned in and kissed him. "I guess I've never said it to you before, but I love you too."

Wes moved back a little and smiled. "Yes, you have." To Bill's quizzical look he said, "Just now, when you said we are a family. Only a man who loves you would say that to you." He paused for a moment and then said quietly, "Bill? Do you know what it costs to go to Stanford?"

"Of course I do. I went to the library and looked it up. It's a lot of money but you'll get a lot of education out of it so it evens out. Look, I make good money and I have invested a lot of it. And Mom left me some. She'd be so happy to know it went to help educate the kind young man who brightened her stay in the nursing home so much."

Wes, with tears in his eyes, went over to the table and picked up another envelope. "There's more. Here."

Bill took the envelope, pulled out the letter inside and read it. When he finished he looked up, tears beginning to form in his eyes. "They think that much of you? A full scholarship? What…"

"Everything. Tuition, books, room and board, everything. For all six years if I don't screw up."

Bill sat down on the couch. Wes went to sit beside him. "What happens if you don't use the room and board? Will they still give you tuition and books or is it a package deal?"

"I don't know. Why?"

"Why? Well, for starters, I don't want to be living all by myself while you're over there living it up with a bunch of handsome college boys. Too much competition."

Wes looked at him for a few moments and then shook his head. "You're going with me? Up there? I thought you would have to stay here, you know, with your job and everything and we'd only get to see each other maybe one weekend a month or something. Oh, Bill, this is wonderful."

"I couldn't do it any other way, Wes. I'll find a job. Mechanics are always in demand. We'll get a little apartment, rent this place out…" He laughed. "I guess with that scholarship the apartment won't have to be so little after all." He kissed Wes again, for a long time. When they broke he said, "Come on, your folks have to be just as anxious about this as we were."

They were. And they were just as happy at the news as Bill and Wes were, especially about the scholarship. "Going to save me a bundle of money," Ken said.

Wes started to say something but caught Bill's eye and stopped. Bill said, "Good. Now you can take Kate on that cruise she's been talking about."

Kate walked into the room just then. "What cruise? The one to Europe?" Ken nodded and she fell into his arms. "Oh, Honey, that's wonderful!" Wes and Bill went into the kitchen when Kate and Ken began kissing.

Pouring himself a Coke, Wes looked at Bill. "You're quite a man, you know that? I think I made the right choice."

Graduation came and Bill thought Wes was the handsomest guy there, especially when he made his valedictorian's speech. That evening he helped Ken and Kate chaperone the school party. Watching the kids at their high-energy dancing, he wondered just how he was going to keep up with Wes. He knew he would but just how was a mystery.

The day before Wes' birthday party, Bill asked him if he'd like to go up to San Francisco for a week as a present. Wes got a big grin on his face but then turned serious. "Can we afford it?"

The 'we' was not lost on Bill. "Look, Wes. For now, let me worry about stuff like that. You worry about school and learning. Once you're out of school and out being a veterinarian, there'll be time enough for you to worry about anything you like. For the next few years though, you just do your job and let me do mine. Okay?"

Wes nodded. "Okay."

Bill kissed him and said, "And yes, we can afford it."

The birthday party was a great success. Ken and Kate put together a barbecue dinner and swim party and Wes invited just the kids he wanted to share his birthday with. Most of the guests were guys but there was a sprinkling of females, too. Bill was introduced as "Wes' friend," with no other explanation. Nobody seemed to care.

Bill was helping Ken at the grill when Ken said, "I guess you're a little excited about going up to San Francisco tomorrow, aren't you. Be a good chance to get to know each other better."

"Yeah," Bill said, turning a hamburger. "I'll finally get to meet Henry."

Ken chuckled. "Is he still calling his dick Henry?"

"He probably always will. I read somewhere that boys who develop pet names like that usually keep them all their lives. They may not admit to them when they're older, but they're there." He turned and looked at Ken. "Hey, he said when he told you about Henry you said you might find a name for yours."

"Yeah, I played with it—excuse the phrasing—but nothing ever seemed right." He grinned. "So it's still just my anonymous penis. You have one?" He laid some hotdogs out so they'd get grill marks.

"No, same as you. He's just my cock."

The 'he' wasn't lost on Ken but before he could say anything a rather muscular young man wearing what appeared to be a light blue posing strap came up and asked if he could help with anything.

"I don't think so, Brad. But check back in half an hour or so and you can help serve this stuff," Ken said.

"Cool. Thanks." The boy turned and sauntered away. The back of whatever he was wearing proved to be nothing but a wide strip of cloth, most of which was hidden in the crack between his cheeks.

"Now there's a boy who likes to show it off. And looks like he has plenty to do it with."

Ken laughed. "Yeah, Brad is something of an exhibitionist. He's over here a lot and if there aren't any females around, he's always the naked one in the pool. I thought he might be gay but Wes says no, he just wants his body to be admired." He lowered his voice. "Wes also said that Brad will let anyone suck his dick as long as they continually tell him how big and handsome it is and how much they want it. I didn't ask if this was from personal experience or not."

Bill laughed. "I hope it was. A guy needs to try out different stuff, learn what turns him on and what doesn't."

Ken thought that Bill was a very realistic man.

In the morning they flew to San Francisco. Bill had bought first-class tickets because it was their very first trip together. As Wes put it, it was the beginning of their life. Singular. Bill did, however, tell Wes not to expect first class every time.

The hotel was gay and turned out to be nicer than Bill had expected. It even had a small restaurant and bar. Their room was bright and airy, the bed was king-sized and the shower would easily accommodate four as long as they were friendly with each other. They had planned to just leave their things in the room and go out for lunch but got sidetracked when Bill pulled Wes into a hug and Wes started unbuttoning Bill's shirt as he kissed him.

They got each other naked and stood, each gazing at the package he'd unwrapped. There was a tentative touch or two and then they were all over each other. They ended up in a sixty-nine position on the bed and brought each other off in under ninety seconds.

When their breathing slowed back to normal, Bill pulled Wes around so he could kiss him. "That wasn't what you'd thought it'd be, was it," Bill said.

Wes nodded. "I thought it would take longer and... I don't know, be different."

"It will be, next time." Bill ran his hand over Wes' stomach. "This time was just for relief, a simple satisfying of a pent-up need to get off. More to calm us down than anything else. Next time it'll be for making love."

They spent some time in the shower and washed each other from hair to toes, with stops in between for licks and kisses. When they were dried off they stood in front of the mirrored closet door, and looked at themselves.

"What do you think?" Bill asked.

Wes turned and looked at him directly. "You're bigger than I thought you'd be."

"Yeah, so are you. Quite a lot bigger." He shrugged. "I'll get used to it. It'll take time. I'll have to spend my whole life at it."

Wes laughed. "Don't worry. I'll help. You have more hair, too." He ran his hand over the hair on Bill's chest. "I knew about this 'cause I've seen you with your shirt off. But this…" He combed Bill's pubic hair with his fingers. "It's so long and silky, not all curled and stiff like mine."

Bill took Wes' scrotum in his hand. "Your balls are so smooth and silky. No hair at all." He moved his hand gently over them, the skin feeling like that of a baby.

"You want balls like that? I can do it for you."

"You can?"

"Sure. We shave them. I do mine every couple of days. I did them this morning because I thought you'd like them that way."

"I do. Where'd you learn that?"

"A guy showed me. His were like that." Wes looked him directly in the eyes. "Bill, is it okay to talk about this? I mean, guys? Before… us?"

Bill chuckled. "Of course it is. Look Wes, everything you've ever done has worked to make you who you are today, this very minute. The same goes for me. If we can't talk about our pasts, we can't really know each other."

Wes stood for a moment, obviously thinking about what Bill had just said. Bill quietly looked at him in the mirror, marveling that this beautiful man was going to be part of him.

"Makes sense," Wes said. "But that has to go for you, too, and you've had a lot more past than I have."

"You'd be surprised, my love. I haven't been a real active guy."

"We'll see about that." He paused for a moment, still looking at Bill directly. "Anyway, this guy, his name was Don or John or something, had these wonderful balls and when I asked him about them he showed me. He took me into the bathroom and shaved mine. Man, they felt so good afterward so," he shrugged, "I've been doing it ever since. We'll do yours the next time we shower if you like."

Bill kissed him. "I like. I love you, but I'd like shaved balls."

They spent the rest of the afternoon slowly bringing each other up to the brink of orgasm and then letting it back off. When Wes finally brought Bill off, he also came himself. It was the first time he'd ever come without touching himself.

That night, after another long session of making love, they went to sleep holding each other. Sometime in the night Bill turned over and Wes snuggled against his back. Bill became half-awake a little later, feeling Wes' erection pressed into his buns. Even in his half-conscious state the idea of taking Wes inside himself excited him. He fell back asleep and into a dream where his name was Henry and he belonged to Wes.

It didn't happen until the next afternoon. They had decided to have a "nap" and were in the shower. Wes went down on his knees and sucked on Bill for a moment before turning him around and kissing his buns. Then he pried them apart and kissed the little pucker he found inside. When he did, Bill sucked in his breath and cried out a little.

"You like that?" Wes asked, his voice muffled by Bill's buns.

"Oh, yeah," Bill groaned. "Oh… yeah."

Wes licked the pucker and then stood up, patting Bill's buns. "Can we do more?" Wes asked, kissing Bill.

"We can do anything you like," Bill answered. "Even that, if you're gentle and go slow."

He was both but Bill could still tell that he was very excited and wanted to hurry it along.

On the bed Wes spent time licking him and then slowly putting his index finger in him. It went in easily so he added a second. He had to be careful with that one because Bill suddenly clamped down on it. "Relax," he whispered, taking Bill's dick into his mouth to redirect his attention. It didn't take long for the third finger to enter Bill and the stretching started. Bill did relax which allowed him to find pleasure in the stretching.

After what seemed a long while, Bill said, "I think I'm ready. Please, Wes? Please come into me, make me part of you."

Wes laid down beside him. "Come up here, Baby. Straddle me." Bill did. "There," Wes said, smearing Henry with lubricant. "I've read in some stories that this is the best way to do it the first time. You can take only as much as you want and only as fast as you want. And I," he added with a grin, taking Bill's dick in his hand, "get to play with him all I want."

Bill bent down and kissed Wes before he started lowering himself. He found that Wes' stretching him had paid off and Henry's head pushed easily into him. As he slowly took more and more into him Wes' face took on an angelic look, one of peace and innocence. When he finally had it all inside him Wes' eyes slowly opened and looked up at Bill.

"I'm going to come, Baby. I can't help it. I'm…"

Bill felt it, all of it, from the first shot to the last. He lost track of how many there were because by the third shot he was coming as well, shooting long ropes of cum, the first of which landed high on the wall behind Wes' head.

Their orgasms hadn't completely played out when Bill felt the urge to start riding Wes, pulling up on him and then settling back down, over and over. The feeling of Wes up inside him was like nothing he'd ever felt before and it was an instant addiction. He knew without any doubt that he would have to have that feeling again and again, for the rest of his life.

It was much the same for Wes. His second orgasm started before the first one was finished. For him, too, it was an immediate addiction. He looked up at Bill, blew him a kiss and closed his eyes, letting the pleasure wash over him.

All in all Wes came four times that afternoon and Bill came three. Afterward they cleaned themselves off and slept in each other's arms for several hours, then showered and went to Fisherman's Wharf for dinner.

In bed that night they talked about the afternoon. They decided that they had to find a better lubricant because the jelly dried out too quickly and was difficult to reapply. They both also wanted to try different positions and they both wanted to try it the other way, Bill inside Wes. But the thing that stood out the most about the afternoon was the pleasure they each— and both together—had experienced. It was another of the many forces that would bind them together.

The next morning, after breakfast, they decided to do some window shopping on the theory that doing so would help them learn more about each other. It worked, too. Wes found out that Bill was very fond of good pens, fond enough that he examined every pen in a display case at Gump's. And Bill discovered that Wes had a deep interest in, and knowledge of, the Art Deco period.

Towards noon, when Bill asked Wes what he'd like for lunch, Wes said, "Nothing. I want to… well, you know."

"I guess I do; at least if that erection you've been carrying around much of the morning is any indication."

Wes laughed. "Is it that obvious?"

"It is to me. But then I'm always looking at it. What're we…"

Wes grinned. "What do you think?"

Bill reached out and patted Wes on the butt. "I think you're going to make me a very happy man, that's what I think."

He did.

It was easier for Wes than for Bill because, although Wes had very limited experience with it, in the past few weeks he'd worked at stretching himself using various vegetables. It was time well spent because when they started, Bill was able to slide into him without any trouble or need to pause. And, as he had done when entering Bill the day before, Wes came almost immediately and, like the day before, that set Bill off.

An hour and a half later, after a shower, they were wrapped up in each other's arms, kissing and touching. "You know," Wes said, "I'd be happy if I could be here like this with you for the rest of my life."

Bill grinned. "I think your stomach might have something to say about that. In fact, I think it just did. You want some lunch?"

Wes stretched and took hold of Bill's dick. "Yeah, I think I do. I just don't want to give up playing with this."

"Shall we call room service? Have the boy bring something up?"

Wes sat up, but didn't relinquish Bill's dick. "That boy, as you call him, has got to be twenty-five or twenty-six. What must you call me?"

Bill leaned in and kissed him. "I don't really call you anything. But I think of you as my equal, and my mate." He thought for a moment, his hand finding and cupping Wes' balls. "I guess I'm guilty of calling most young guys I don't know 'boys' but I don't mean it in a negative way. For me it's just an affectionate way to refer to them." He tightened his grip on Wes' balls to just the pressure he'd found turned Wes on. He was rewarded by a low groan and an erection sprouting just above his hand. "Okay?"

Wes nodded. "If we're going to have lunch, you'd better stop that."

They ended up with a compromise. They ordered several plates of finger food and after the "boy" who had delivered it left, feeding it to each other with Bill straddling Wes who was on his back, Henry deep inside Bill.

––––––––––––

During their stay in San Francisco they rented a car and went down the peninsula to Palo Alto where they were given a tour of the university campus. The housing office had lots and lots of listings for off-campus housing so they figured they'd have little trouble finding a place in August.

Back in Phoenix Wes moved in with Bill and they were suddenly a "real couple." Even Ken and Kate, Wes' parents, began to think of them that way and were happy for them. Wes introduced Bill to some of his friends and Bill did the same for Wes. There were a few raised eyebrows on both sides but for the most part each was accepted by the other's friends.

Wes spent the summer working at the local animal shelter, mainly cleaning cages but learning as well. He quickly became invaluable to the shelter and they were sorry to see him leave in August to go up to Stanford.

As predicted, they had little trouble finding a nice apartment in Palo Alto, near enough to the campus that on nice days, Wes could walk to his classes. Bill found a job with the local Cadillac dealer and fit right in with the other guys. He made no effort to hide the fact that he lived with a man, a student, and it was quickly understood that they were a unit.

Six years of college went by far faster than either of them would have thought and May of 1998 arrived well before they were ready for it. Wes graduated third in his veterinary class and received several offers of a job almost immediately. The one in Palm Springs intrigued him the most so in early May they flew down to check the place out.

"I'm sorry you've been stuck with making all the arrangements," Wes said on the way down. "I guess things just got away from me."

Bill looked at him. "Yeah, I guess being third in your class can do that to a guy. Also getting more job offers than anyone else."

Wes smiled and put his hand on top of Bill's. "Thank you, Baby. Because of you I've had it so damn much easier than most of the kids." He looked out the window. "You think we'll like it in Palm Springs?"

Bill shrugged. "It'll be more like Phoenix than Palo Alto, I can tell you that. But yeah, I think we will."

They did. They loved it and on the tenth of May, 1998, they bought the house at Number 29 Taylor Circle. They moved in on the first of June.

TAYLOR CIRCLE

The neighborhood proved to be more friendly than they had expected, knowing that the neighbors were mainly senior citizens. The first ones they met were Mike and Samantha Spraker, who lived next door to the south at Number 15. The Sprakers made a rather formal call the day after Wes and Bill moved in. Mrs. Spraker presented them with a tuna casserole because, she said, "When you're just getting settled you don't need to cook, too." She was a little surprised to find that there was no Mrs. Benson in residence and even more surprised to find that there was no Mrs. Benson, period. To her credit, though, when told there was no Mrs. Davis either, she figured out Wes and Bill's relationship immediately. Mr. Spraker, on the other hand, hadn't a clue. He figured they were just a couple of bachelors living the good life. More power to you, he thought, but didn't say out loud where his wife might hear.

The second neighbor they met was Mr. Brown, who lived, with his wife, Mrs. Brown, next door to the east, at Number 50. He rang their doorbell late on the morning of their second day. He came bearing one of his wife's homemade apple pies and figured out Bill and Wes before he was in the door.

"Welcome to the neighborhood," Mr. Brown said, handing the pie to Wes. "You'll be the first queers we've had here." Wes saw the fire come into Bill's eyes and immediately went to the kitchen with the pie. Bill did not take easily to being called "queer."

"Well, you know," Bill said with a smile, "for us it's the first time we've lived next door to niggers so I guess we're kind of even."

Mr. Brown didn't even hear that last part. "Who the hell you think you are, callin' me that?"

Bill shrugged but never stopped smiling. "Well, I figured that if you choose to call us by the most offensive word you can think of then courtesy demands that I do the same to you."

They stood and glared at each other for a minute or more, but unlike most confrontations, each of the men was actually thinking about what had just happened. Mr. Brown broke the silence first.

"That true? You people find bein' called queer offensive?"

"Yes, sir. As offensive as you find being called a nig…" He stopped. "You know? I find that word so personally offensive that I can't even say it. Please forgive me."

Mr. Brown looked closely at him and decided that he was sincere. "I'll forgive you if you'll forgive me. What should I call you guys?"

Bill smiled at him. "Gay is probably best."

Mr. Brown stuck out his hand. "Glad to meet you, Mr. Gay Man. I think we'll get along."

"Thank you, Mr. Black Man. If we think about things, I know we will." He turned his head and raised his voice. "It's okay, Wes. You can come back now."

"You guys want a beer?" Wes called from the kitchen. "I'm having one."

Bill smiled. "You like one, Mr. Brown? I think I would."

"Skip the mister, hey? Everyone call me just Brown. And yes indeed, I would like a beer, that is if you won't tell Mrs. Brown about it. She don't approve of me drinkin' beer much."

Wes came out of the kitchen carrying three chilled mugs. "It's our secret, Brown."

They did become friends, or at least friendly neighbors. Brown took to showing up in the afternoon when Bill drew the early shift and on weekends when he could hear them working in the back yard. He always accepted a beer, if offered, but never asked for one. Wes figured that if Mrs. Brown smelled it on his breath, Brown could say that he had a beer just to be neighborly.

One Wednesday afternoon after they'd been on Taylor Circle for a couple of months, Brown showed up with five or six little snapdragon plants. "Mrs. Brown, she likes 'em so I built her a little box outside her kitchen window and planted some. I guess I bought too many so I thought you might like them."

"Well, thank you, Brown. Wes is very fond of these so I'll plant them just outside the bedroom. Now, can I get you a beer? This one's gone," he held up an obviously empty bottle, "and I was just about to get me another and then take a swim."

"Well," Brown chuckled, "I couldn't turn down a neighborly offer like that, could I?"

Bill laughed and went to get the beer. He'd found that he'd kind of taken to Brown. The man didn't have much education but what he did have was a lot of common sense and always an interesting point of view. He read the newspaper every day, seemingly from the front page through the local news to the comics, and knew a great deal about what was going on in the world.

"Here we go," Bill said, handing Brown a green bottle. "It's the good stuff." Wes had a taste for Heinekens so Bill saw to it that it was generally in the house. "Hey, I was just going to have a swim. You want to join me?"

"Me? No." Brown shook his head but looked longingly at the pool. "Not 'cept if you might have a spare bathing suit around."

Bill looked at him, wondering what that meant. "Don't need a suit, Brown. Hasn't been one in that pool since we moved in except when Wes's mother was here." A sudden thought occurred to him. "Unless maybe you're uncomfortable swimming naked with a gay man or something."

Brown looked him in the eye and laughed. "Ain't that. It's Mrs. Brown. She don't approve of swimmin' naked, 'specially in her back yard pool."

Bill held up his hand and closed down one finger for each of his points. "First of all, this isn't Mrs. Brown's back yard pool. It's Wes' and mine. Second, what Mrs. Brown doesn't know won't hurt you. Third, I honestly don't believe we have any swimming suits around, much less a spare one. And last but not least, it's a damn hot day and that water looks very cool and inviting." He took a swig of his beer. "So what d'ya say?"

Brown didn't hesitate. He pulled off his shirt and started on his belt. When they were both naked he looked at Bill and said, "Hey! You almost big as me."

Bill followed his eyes. "This?" He took hold of his dick and waved it around.

"Yeah. I'm the black man here. Black guys are always the biggest."

"Uh… You haven't been around many naked men, have you, Brown?"

He thought for a moment. "Can't say as I have but everybody knows the black guy is always the biggest. Ask anyone."

"Well," Bill said, sliding into the pool, "I guess maybe I've had more experience with this than you have so I can say with some confidence that that isn't always true. I've seen some really big black guys, guys who would put us both to shame, but I've seen some who are smaller than me, too."

"Ain't fair," Brown mumbled as he walked gingerly down the steps into the water. "Ain't fair at all. Man, this do feel good." He turned on his back and let himself float.

Lord, Bill thought, what'll he do when he sees Wes?

They spent a pleasant half hour in the pool before Brown decided it was time to get home to Mrs. Brown.

Later, when Wes came in, Bill was just putting the finishing touches on a coq au vin. Wes kissed him and said, "Man, I'm sure glad you got bored while I was in school and took that cooking class. I'll bet we eat better than anyone."

Bill patted him on the ass. "Oh, I don't know. That pie Mrs. Brown sent over was pretty good. Oh, speaking of Mrs. Brown, her husband was over here this afternoon. Brought some snapdragon plants which I planted by the bedroom door."

"Oh, thank you. I love snapdragons."

Bill patted him again. "I know you do. Anyway, it was a hot afternoon so I gave Brown a beer and suggested a swim."

"He take you up on it? I mean, would he take his clothes off with a gay man?"

"Yup, he's come a long way. At first he wanted to borrow a bathing suit but I told him we didn't have any so he got with the program and took his clothes off."

"And…"

"And he informed me that it wasn't fair that my dick is almost, almost mind you, as big as his. He claims that black men are always bigger than white guys." He began to giggle. "All I could think of was what'll happen when he gets a load of you!"

Wes laughed. "Oh, come on, I'm not that big."

"Yes you are that big. And he's going to have a seizure if he ever sees you hard, that's for sure. Now, go take a shower and set the table."

———

A couple of nights later Bill and Wes were awakened by a commotion in the street outside. They pulled on some pants and went to see what was going on. In the street, in front of Number 78, they found a fire truck and an ambulance. Later they learned that the fire truck is always dispatched when the paramedics go out on a call.

In this case the call was from Millie Jordan, Brown's next-door neighbor. Jack, her husband, had become violently ill just after one o'clock and she couldn't lift him out of their bed so she called for help. The paramedics determined that he'd had a mild heart attack and took him to the hospital. Wes ran back to the house and got one of his cards. He wrote their home number on it and when he gave it to Millie he told her to call any time she needed anything.

A few days later, on a Sunday, she rang their doorbell and asked them to help her get Jack out of their car and into the house. They did, and found Jack weak as a newborn baby. When they got him into the house and into bed, Millie couldn't thank them enough. For the next week Bill took some sort of cooked food over to them every day, and Millie was even more thankful.

On the Sunday after, Brown came over bearing another one of Mrs. Brown's pies, this time strawberry. "Well, thank you," Bill said, accepting the pie. "We really appreciate this. I'll take half of it over to the Jordan's if you won't mind." He laughed. "And don't worry, Mrs. Brown will get full credit. I won't try to pass it off as mine," he paused for a second, "as if I could."

Brown shrugged. "Not necessary. I just come from delivering the very same pie to them. Mrs. Brown is right worried about them, says he don't look good at all. She's kinda pale, too."

Since Wes was out in the pool, Bill debated taking Brown out there but then thought: What the heck, it'll happen sometime so why not now? "Hey, Brown," he said, getting a beer out of the refrigerator, "you want to go for a swim? Wes is already in the pool and I was just going there myself."

"Hey, yeah, good day for a swim."

So they went outside, stripped down and got in the pool. While they were lazily swimming around, Bill caught Brown looking at Wes a couple of times but nothing was said until they got out to dry off.

"Hey, Wesley, you ever looked into your ancestors? Like your family tree?"

Wes shook his head. "Can't say that I have, Brown. I knew all of my grandparents but that's as far as it goes. Why?"

"'cause I'm here to tell you, you got a black man somewhere back there. Ain't no white guy with a dick big as that one you're carrying around who doesn't. You go down to the library sometime and look it up. I guarantee you'll find him." Wes smiled. "No, really," Brown went on, "he's there. I guarantee it."

Wes nodded. "Could be, Brown, could very well be. One of these days I'll do that, go look it up. I'll let you know. You want another beer? I think I'll have one."

Brown finished drying his dick and pulled the foreskin back over the head. "Sure, I'd like that."

"Me, too," Bill spoke up. "And, if you want, there's some guacamole in the fridge. Bring that and some corn chips, will you?"

They spent the rest of the day sitting naked by the pool, Brown taking occasional glances at Wes and almost imperceptibly shaking his head.

For the rest of the summer Brown visited often on weekends, sitting naked under the umbrella, never having more than two beers and always having something interesting to say. Mrs. Brown, who of course knew all about the beers, figured it was good for him to socialize with other men, and white men at that. And he never, ever, came home the least bit intoxicated. That made her happiest. She didn't know that they sat around naked and that they swam the same way too, but if she had she probably wouldn't have minded that, either. Just as long as they didn't do it in her back yard.

In late September Jack Jordan died. Fortunately he was in the hospital at the time or, as Millie confided to Wes, she could never have slept in their bed again. As it was, she slept on the living room couch for nearly two weeks.

The day the "For Sale" sign went up, Bill went over and asked Millie what she was doing.

"Well," she said, "my son has asked me to come and live with them in Wichita. His wife agreed and," she smiled here, "got on the phone herself to tell me so. I think it'll be better for me, too. Not so much housework when there's two doing it."

"We're going miss you around here," Bill said. "Why don't you come over for dinner tonight and tell us all about it? Wes will be interested, I know."

Millie did go over for dinner, as she did several more times in the next weeks, talking about her preparations and what the real estate man said about the people who came to look at her house. When it sold she couldn't wait to tell them.

"It's two men," she said over a pre-dinner cocktail. "They're very nice. One's a lawyer, I think, and the other manages Lawton's. You know, the big department store? They're both quite handsome, from San Francisco. I think they're…" she searched for the word but couldn't find it, "well, they're like you, you know?"

They did. And so Number 78 Taylor Circle was bought by Buzz Clark and Mickey O'Rourke, Taylor Circle's second gay couple.

CHAPTER TWO

BUZZ & MICKEY

Buzz and Mickey met in San Francisco on a chilly February evening, around nine-thirty. They were on Polk Street, both pretending to look in a store window at a display of very with-it shoes. What they were actually doing, of course, was using the window as a mirror so they could study each other. Each knew what the other was doing, and the more they looked, the more each hoped that something was going to come of it.

"How do you suppose people walk in heels like those?" Mickey asked.

"I have no idea," Buzz replied, looking at Mickey directly and noticing for the first time that he seemed to have an erection. "When I was nineteen my dad bought me a pair of riding boots, you know, cowboy boots with heels? It took me weeks to learn to walk properly in them. And they were only an inch and a half. Those," he pointed to a bright pink creation, "are five inches at the very least."

"Did you ride? I mean, horses?" Mickey looked him up and down and liked what he saw. It was also not lost on him that Buzz was looking directly at his crotch. He wondered if his erection showed.

"Yeah, sometimes. We lived in El Paso for a time and my dad insisted that we learn. I hated it but my brother took to it big time. He lives on a farm in Iowa now and rides all the time." He figured it was his turn. "You ever ridden a horse?"

Mickey shivered but tried to hide it. The fog was getting thicker. "No. I rode the little ponies that came to town with the circus a few times but I don't think that counts, does it? I was all of seven."

"Anything counts if you want it to. Even ponies." The more Buzz looked at Mickey the more he wanted him. "You live around here?"

Mickey was relieved; he wasn't very good at this and was glad Buzz had taken the lead. "Up the hill, on Sacramento Street." He pretended the idea just occurred to him: "Hey, you want to come up, maybe have a drink?"

"Yeah, I'd like that."

They'd each done this, or something like it, a fair number of times before but even so, something about this time seemed different. Mickey hoped it wasn't going to be a disaster, like with that cute kid who tried to rob him afterwards. Buzz hoped it was going to last the whole night and that he wasn't going to find himself out in the fog at three in the morning, looking for a cab.

It wasn't a disaster, for either one of them. First of all, their very first kiss sparked something special in each of them. They'd each had encounters where sexual interest was high, some even where lust boiled over and they didn't even make it to the bedroom but this was somehow different.

Second, their sexual compatibility was near one hundred percent. When Buzz patted Mickey on the ass he didn't even have to ask if he could go there. He knew he could and that he'd be most welcome. But they started slow, sipping a drink while they undressed each other. They spent time fondling each other, touching each other's bodies, which of course led to kissing, which led to licking, which led to sucking. It was near three o'clock before they got to the main event and, even so, managed to stretch that out until after four. Then they slept, Buzz pressed against Mickey's back, his arms around him, his fingers splayed out in the silky hair on his chest. They slept well.

They woke a little before ten. Without shyness or coyness they got out of bed, Mickey's erection pointing towards the bathroom and Buzz's pointing towards the ceiling. They stood on either side of the toilet and relieved themselves, each unabashedly watching the other. Mickey handed Buzz a new toothbrush and they brushed, and then gargled and then went back to bed where they made love to each other again.

Later, when nature called, Buzz went into the bathroom and took care of it without closing the door. When he got back in bed Mickey kissed him and said, "You didn't close the door."

Buzz smiled and said, "Yeah."

"Why? I mean, guys always do."

Buzz sat up and gathered Mickey into his arms. "Because I don't have to. With you."

Mickey thought about it for more than a minute. Then he kissed Buzz and said, "Yeah. You don't." When it was his call, he didn't close the door either.

Around noon serious hunger was setting in so Mickey made French toast and bacon. Afterward they washed the dishes together, Buzz washing and Mickey drying and putting away. Then they went back to bed.

A little later, when Buzz was fully inside Mickey, he said, "You know, when I'm inside you it feels like nothing I've ever felt before. Kind of like... Well, like I, or really, my dick I guess, belongs there. You make me part of you. Does that make any sense?"

In a quiet voice Mickey said, "Push in. As far as you can. Please?"

Buzz had been holding back some. His dick was fairly big and the first two inches of it flared out sharply making the base extremely thick. Most guys he went to bed with complained that the base was too thick and painfully stretched them too far so he had learned to hold back and not try to hit bottom. He did that now, slowly, and he felt Mickey accept him while his inside walls seemed to contract around him.

A low moan escaped Mickey and he quietly said, "Dear God in Heaven." Then he came. Big time. After, he was silent for a bit and then twisted his head around so Buzz could kiss him. "That was the most incredible thing," he said into Buzz's mouth. He pushed back against him.

Buzz got the message and began stroking in him again. He was close but not quite ready when Mickey said it again. "Now! Push in, as far as you can." Buzz did and again, there was that sensation of everything contracting around his dick, enclosing him while Mickey moaned into the pillow.

At the end, when Buzz couldn't control it anymore and fell over his edge, without thinking he pushed in deep and it happened again and even though Buzz was in the throes of his own orgasm, he knew it was happening.

When their breathing finally evened out and Buzz slipped out, Mickey looked into his eyes and said, "You do belong there. It's like your dick was made especially for me."

"Did... did you really come?"

Mickey rolled up on his side, uncovering a huge wet spot on the sheet. He nodded his head. "Yeah, I did. Three times... 'cause you... I don't know, you do something to me, inside me." He shook his head. "Three times. I've never done that before."

They had a shower and changed the bed. Then Mickey opened a bottle of wine and they got back into bed and started talking.

"You know something weird?" Mickey said, touching his wineglass to Buzz's. "You just made me come three times and I don't even know your name."

"Yeah, is that gay or what? It's Buzz. Buzz Clark."

Mickey kissed him. "Pleased to meet you, Buzz Clark. I'm Mickey O'Rourke. I'm twenty-five years old and I work in men's sportswear at Macy's. Originally I'm from Portland, Oregon."

Buzz kissed him back. "I'm twenty-seven and work for Pillsbury, Madison, Sutro as a junior lawyer. I'm from all over the place, Texas, Indiana, New York, you name it. My dad liked to move around a lot." He laughed. "When I was a teenager I had this fantasy that my dad was some kind of fugitive and we had to keep moving to stay ahead of the law. I even checked the Wanted posters every time I went into the post office, just to see if he was there. It turned out that he and my mom both had itchy feet and just wanted to see the country."

They talked about their jobs, their aspirations and the last movie each had seen. They made love again. What finally drove them out of bed was a different hunger.

They went to a gay restaurant because they didn't want to quit holding hands. They had a good dinner but didn't taste much of it. What they tasted was something sweeter than food although they didn't yet understand the significance of it. After dinner they went back to Mickey's and messed up the sheets again.

The next morning they did the gay thing and went to brunch. They had Bloody Marys and ate eggs Benedict, just like, as gay men, they were supposed to. After, they walked around downtown and pointed out things in windows that they'd someday like to have. Considering the difference in their backgrounds, their tastes were remarkably similar.

When they tired of walking Buzz said, "Let's go to my place this time."

"Yeah. We'll have clean sheets," Mickey said with a laugh.

They actually went back to Mickey's first so he could get the clothes he would need to go to work the next day. Doing this seemed so natural that it never occurred to either of them that it was a statement of intent on both their parts.

Buzz's apartment turned out to be somewhat larger than Mickey's and had an actual bedroom where Mickey's was a studio. "Nice place," Mickey said. "Big and with a view, too."

Buzz kissed him. "Yeah, I moved in a couple of months ago after I got a raise. I really like it."

"Me, too."

Before they went to bed Mickey asked for a towel which he folded in two and put over the sheet on his side of the bed. "Don't want to have to change the sheets," he said with a laugh.

Buzz gave him a quizzical look. "Do you do that every time? Come, I mean, when a guy is inside you and presses really hard?"

"You know what, Buzz? It's never happened to me before. It's something you do, inside me." He shrugged. "I think it means you're supposed to be there. But you know what? I like to be the top guy too, sometimes."

Buzz smiled. "I thought you might—or at least I hoped you might 'cause I like to be the one with the dick inside him once in a while." He pulled Mickey into a tight hug. "Like now."

It was another case of a perfect fit. Mickey prepared him well and then slid into him with no effort at all. Buzz liked it on his back, with his legs on Mickey's shoulders, so he could watch Mickey. Mickey liked it that way because he could play with Buzz's dick. All in all it was an extremely satisfying way to spend the afternoon.

That evening they went to a restaurant reputed to have the best-looking waiters in town. The place lived up to its reputation, but Mickey and Buzz hardly noticed. Over cocktails Mickey asked Buzz if he could cook.

"Well," Buzz said, "I can fry an egg and make fair coffee. Oh, yeah, and I'm a whiz with the microwave." He spread his arms. "What can I say, I eat out a lot. How about you? Do you know the stove from the refrigerator?"

Mickey laughed. "Yeah. the stove is the one with the little knobs on it." Buzz laughed and Mickey went on. "Actually I do know my way around a kitchen a little bit. My mom thought it would be good if we kids knew how to get along in the world so she taught us enough about cooking so we could survive." He grinned. "She also taught us to do the laundry and iron a shirt.

Then she got dad to show us how to balance a checkbook. So you see? I'm a domestic whiz kid."

"That's good, because I'm sure not. I'll tell you a little secret. I haven't balanced my checkbook since I opened the account. I just take what the bank says and don't argue."

Mickey turned serious for a moment. "I guess that's okay. I mean if the bank makes a mistake it's usually thousands of dollars and I guess you'd probably notice it. But you really should balance it."

"Are you volunteering?"

Mickey grinned. "Probably."

After dinner they walked back to Buzz's apartment, holding hands most of the way. At the apartment they took their shoes off and sat on the couch, watching the late news and playing footsy. Then they decided it was getting late and they should get some sleep.

Once in bed, of course, the idea of sleep seemed pointless. Buzz pulled Mickey tight against him and whispered, "My turn again." They lay on their sides so Buzz could hang on to Mickey's dick.

"I love the way you do this, Buzz."

"What do you mean? How else can you do it?"

"Well, some guys just want to get it over with. They do it fast and don't care about anything but getting off. You do it like you enjoy getting there, too."

"I do. As they say, 'Getting there is half the fun.' Only it's not. It's more like three quarters or ninety percent." He pressed into Mickey just as far as he could. When nothing happened he pulled back and then tried it again. "I guess it isn't going to work all the time, is it?" He sounded disappointed.

"Wait." Mickey grabbed the towel he'd put beside the bed and then turned on his stomach, pulling Buzz with him. When Buzz pressed in again he was rewarded with a long growl and then the spasms of orgasm.

When he could talk again Mickey said, "Maybe it only works when I'm on my belly." He paused and then said, "Again?"

Buzz happily accommodated him.

The next week went by pretty smoothly. On Tuesday Mickey needed a clean shirt and they found that Buzz's clothes fit him as well as they did Buzz. By Friday Mickey was dressed completely in Buzz's clothes, including the shoes.

Mickey found his way around Buzz's kitchen but found that Buzz had practically nothing in the way of pots, pans and tools. Things began appearing as he used his employee discount at the store.

On Friday they each had a gift for the other, to mark their first week's "anniversary." Mickey gave Buzz an outfit: pants, jacket, shirt, tie, socks and shoes. Buzz was delighted and had to try on each article immediately.

"Hey, you forgot the underwear," Buzz said, pulling on the pants.

Mickey snapped his fingers. "Damn, I did. You may have noticed I hardly ever wear it and I just forgot. Let's see how you look."

When Buzz was dressed Mickey looked at him critically and then laughed.

"And what's funny?"

"I see why you wear underwear, now. That is one big hose you're hiding in those pants."

Buzz looked down. "Not really. It's the way I'm built, way high on my abdomen so it pushes out rather than hanging between my legs like a lot of guys. I've always been self- conscious about it."

Mickey ran his hand over it. "Don't be. It's too pretty to hide."

Dinner was delayed by an hour or so.

After dinner, sitting on the couch with a glass of wine, Buzz handed Mickey a small, blue box. It said Tiffany on the top and inside was a silver key chain and a shiny new key. "It fits the downstairs door as well as the apartment. I figure if we're going to live here you need a key."

Mickey looked at him. "We're going to live here?"

Buzz laughed. "Unless you want to live in your studio. Or maybe we should look for a totally new place. You know, something we'd both pick out."

Mickey just looked at him.

After a moment Buzz leaned in and kissed him. "I know this is fast and I guess I forgot to mention that I've fallen in love with you, but look, we're good together, in bed and out, and I, for one, don't want to lose a single minute of that. Okay?"

Mickey nodded. "Okay." There was a long silence and then: "Buzz? What just happened?"

Buzz kissed him again. "I just proposed to you and you just accepted."

"I thought that was it. But something was left out."

"What?"

Mickey put his arms around Buzz and laid his head against Buzz's chest. "The fact that I've fallen in love with you, too." He looked up. "I love you, Buzz Clark."

"I love you, Mickey O'Rourke. For now and forever."

And so, in the space of one week, Buzz and Mickey became a family. The rest took considerably longer, as life generally does.

They decided to stay at Buzz's until the lease ran out and then look for a new place. It turned out, however that they grew used to the place and lived there for seven years, until they bought a house of their own.

Life was, of course, not without its hurdles. It never is when two very different people become a single unit, no matter how much they love each other. The first one came right after Mickey gave up his studio apartment. He was sending out a few change-of-address notices, one to the skin magazine he subscribed to and a couple to his family.

"Hey," Buzz said, watching him work and wishing he'd finish so they could go to bed and play, "don't forget the Registrar of Voters. Just address it to them at City Hall."

"Why? I'm not registered."

Buzz was shocked. "Not registered to vote? Oh, sweetheart, you have to be registered. Otherwise you can't vote."

Mickey shrugged. It had never seemed important to him. It was very important to Buzz. There ensued a discussion of civic responsibilities which was mostly a lecture on Buzz's part. They finally did go to bed but skipped the playing that night.

They made up for it the next morning and both of them were late for work. That night Buzz brought home a voter registration form which Mickey filled out. He never missed voting in an election after that.

The second hurdle was much bigger and far more important to their lives. One night, after they'd been together for about a year and a half, Buzz, over dinner, said, "Hey, guess who got a blow job today."

Mickey looked up. "Who?"

"Me, silly," Buzz laughed. "In the men's room down in the parking garage. I went in to pee and some guy came in right after me and took the urinal next to me. He started to play with himself, had a nice dick, and stood back, showing it to me. Seeing him like that made me hard too and the next thing I know he's on his knees with my dick in his mouth."

"In the parking garage? Isn't that dangerous?"

"I guess. But maybe not. I don't think anybody ever goes there. Well, except for this guy."

"And you. You were there. Did you come?"

"Man, did I ever. I think that took longer than building up to it. The guy was good."

There was a long silence. Then: "Buzz? Do you do that often? Get blown in a men's room?"

Buzz knew something was wrong but honestly couldn't figure out what it was. Sure, he'd done it a few times, but this was the first since he and Mickey got together. It didn't mean anything to him except it was a surprise orgasm in the middle of the day. "Uh, no. Not since... Is something wrong?"

Mickey shrugged. "No. No, I just have a lot on my mind. From work. It'll... it'll be okay."

Buzz got up, went around the table and kissed him. "Anything I can help with?"

"No. Maybe later, I don't know. Eat your dinner."

They went to bed early but didn't have sex. Mickey seemed restless but Buzz chalked it up to whatever was going on at work.

It was the same in the morning but both of them pretended not to notice. When they left for work their kiss was dry and perfunctory.

Mickey had a meeting first thing that morning and couldn't seem to keep his mind on anything. When it was over, Jason, manager of the electronics department and a good friend, caught him by the arm. "Coffee? I think you could use some."

Mickey nodded. He knew he'd been quiet in the meeting, something he rarely was, but he just couldn't get Buzz's blow job out of his mind. "Sure, might as well."

Instead of the employee lounge they went out of the building to a little coffee shop down the street. When they were settled with their coffee and a couple of Danish, Jason said, "Okay, out with it. What's bothering you?"

Mickey stirred his coffee and decided What the hell? "Buzz. He told me last night that he got a blow job from some guy in a men's room."

Jason sipped his coffee. "So?"

Mickey just stared at him.

"Uh oh, is that outside your rules?" Jason picked up one of the Danishes and looked at it critically. He put it aside.

"What rules?"

"I don't know what you call them. We call them our rules of behavior." He picked up the Danish again and then looked up. "Don't tell me you guys don't have rules, you know, what you can and can't do? Have you guys even talked about this stuff?"

Mickey was mystified. "Talked about what stuff."

Jason put the Danish back on its plate. "Well, like sex. I mean, there's more to it than that but the sex part usually comes up first."

Mickey shook his head. "Should we? Have these… rules?"

"Well, lots of guys don't but it sure makes life easier when you do. With rules you both know what you can and can't do." He picked up the Danish again. "Ours are pretty simple. Like sex: unless one of us is away, if we have sex with someone else we do it as a team, together."

This was an entirely new concept to Mickey. He'd figured if you're with somebody then he's the only one you have sex with. He said as much to Jason.

"Well," Jason said, "that works for some guys, I guess, but it sure wouldn't work for us. Face it, Mickey, we're men. Men like to get off. Doesn't matter if it's with our own hand or some other guy's mouth, we like getting our rocks off." He took a bite out of the Danish, made a face, put the Danish back on its plate and pushed it away. "I'll tell you something, Mickey. You and Buzz need a long talk and you need it now, or things are going to go up like an atom bomb one of these days."

Mickey reached for the second Danish but Jason pushed the plate away. "They're terrible. Drink your coffee. We have to get going."

Mickey thought about it for the rest of the day, pretty much ignoring the men's sportswear department. He left work early and stopped at a restaurant they liked and bought two crab salads to go.

At home, when Buzz came in, he was carrying several take-out boxes from a Chinese restaurant they often went to. When he saw the table set he looked at Mickey. "Chow mein, fried shrimp, pot stickers and steamed buns," he said, putting the boxes down on the counter.

Mickey opened the refrigerator. "Crab salads, garlic bread and white wine."

There was a long moment of silence while they looked at each other and a longer one while they held each other. After a bit Buzz said quietly, "You must know that blow job in the parking garage didn't mean anything to me. I mean, nothing more than jerking off in the shower, which I'm pretty sure you know I do sometimes."

Mickey nodded. "Yeah, sometimes I wish we had a clear shower curtain so I could watch. That would be so sexy, watching you jerk off."

Buzz stepped back. "Get one. That would be so exciting, knowing you were watching me." He paused and Mickey could see that he was sprouting an erection. "I could watch you, too, couldn't I? God, that would be sexy."

The idea was giving Mickey a hard-on too and he thought they'd better get to talking or they'd end up in bed. He turned to the sink. "Crab or Chinese?"

"Crab salads. We can warm up the Chinese tomorrow. You want a drink first?"

They had their drink, two of them actually, and talked. It was the beginning of a dialog that would last for years, off and on, as their lives and needs changed. For the moment, though, it was enough to clear the air, make some mutually agreeable rules and solidify their partnership.

———————

Over the years they both did good things outside their life together. Buzz got more and more responsibility at the law firm and with that responsibility came more and more money.

Mickey got promoted, first to department manager, then floor manager and, finally, store manager. He was good at retail, good at figuring out what would engage the public, and good at figuring out what wouldn't. He built the men's department into the largest and most profitable in the Bay Area.

Then, on a cold, blustery night in December, they became a family of three. Buzz woke up around two, hearing a strange noise. He could barely hear it over the wind but there was something and Buzz knew he had to find out what it was or he would never go back to sleep. He got up quietly, so as not to disturb Mickey, and slowly walked around the house. The noise was loudest in the bathroom, seeming to come from the window. Buzz looked out but didn't see anything. On a hunch he opened the window and there it was: a sopping wet blob of gray fur with yellow eyes and a soft, pitiful cry.

Buzz brought it in and wrapped it in a hand towel, both to dry it off and to give it warmth. "Well, well, who do we have here?" he said, looking directly in the kitten's eyes. "You aren't very old yet, are you?"

He took it to the kitchen and found a small box in which he wadded up a couple of dishtowels. He laid the kitten in it and the kitten immediately stretched and meowed.

"You're hungry, aren't you, little guy? Well, let's see what we can find." What he found was a can of tuna which, when he put some of it down, the kitten ate like it hadn't eaten for a long time.

Next Buzz tore up yesterday's San Francisco Chronicle and scattered it in a box he found. "This'll have to do for a kitty box until we can get something better," he said. He put the kitten in the box and the kitten cooperated by doing what kittens do after eating. Buzz yawned and put the kitten back in the box with the towels, where it promptly curled up and went to sleep. Buzz said good-night to it and went back to bed himself.

Some three hours later he woke again to a strange noise, only this time it was much, much louder. When he opened his eyes, the first thing he saw was Mickey, looking at him. "I wondered how long it would take for you to wake up," Mickey said.

"What…" He turned and there, on his pillow, was a little ball of gray fur purring loudly enough for two cats. He leaned over it and kissed Mickey.

"Where did it come from?" Mickey asked, his hand reaching along the bed to find what was always there when Buzz first woke up.

"Outside. He, or she, I don't know, was on the sill of the bathroom window, soaked and cold. Last I saw it was asleep in a box in the kitchen."

"And you thought it would stay there? Sleeping all by itself in a box? Hardly."

"Why not? It had food. And a place to go to the bathroom. What…"

"Companionship, sweetheart." His hand found what it was looking for and slid along the length of it. Involuntarily it flexed and seemed to puff up.

"You better stop that," Buzz said, "or kitty will see his first blow job."

Mickey eased the covers down and swung himself around. "But it won't be the last one if he stays here." He didn't say more since he didn't like to talk with his mouth full.

A little later Buzz called his secretary and told him he was taking the day off. Then, after Mickey had gone, he found a veterinarian in the yellow pages who could see him—and the gray ball of fluff—that morning.

When Mickey got home that evening Buzz greeted him with a kiss and a martini. They took their drinks into the living room where Mickey found a five foot high "Kitty Condo" standing by the window. The gray ball of fluff was sprawled out on the highest part, surveying the room.

"What'd the vet say?"

Buzz sat on the couch and patted the place beside him. "Well, he's a boy and he's somewhere between six and eight weeks old. He's healthy except for the ear mites which Dr. Adams said all outdoor cats have. He put some stuff in his ears and the mites will be gone in a couple of days."

Mickey got up from the couch and walked over to the Kitty Condo and reached out to pet the kitten who immediately turned on his back, spread his four legs and started to purr.

"Yeah, he likes his belly rubbed." He came over and demonstrated. The kitten began to purr louder.

Mickey laughed. "You've bonded to him faster than you bonded to me."

"Not really. I knew I wanted to keep you by that first morning. I just had to figure out how to convince you."

"Well," Mickey said, running his hand gently over Buzz's crotch, "you had a very effective way of doing it. And the nice thing is, you keep doing it, over and over." He turned and gave Buzz a long kiss. "What are we going to call him?"

"I thought we might call him Harry. You know, because he is. Only with two 'r's, not an 'i.'"

Mickey laughed again. "Well, I'm sure he will appreciate that. The spelling, I mean. So Harry it is." He rubbed Harry's belly. "Welcome to the family, guy." He was rewarded with a little nuzzle and a loud purr.

So Harry came to live with them. They put an ad for a found kitten in the neighborhood paper and spent two weeks hoping no one would answer it. No one did.

They did some traveling, too, and bought a house. Their sex life got better and better as well. Buzz still got the occasional blow job somewhere but he always told Mickey about it and often demonstrated it as well. Mickey grew quite confident that these meant nothing to Buzz except a quick, easy orgasm, just like jerking off in the shower or when he was bored.

Mickey, on the other hand, didn't have much of any sex other than with Buzz although there was that one day Buzz dragged him down to the parking garage and made him go into the men's room and stay there until someone came in and took care of him. He waited all of three minutes before a man came in and stood at the urinal next to him. The whole thing took under five minutes and Mickey had an explosive orgasm.

Mickey did like it, though, when he and Buzz found the occasional someone—or better yet, a couple—who wanted to bed the two of them together. That, he thought, was great fun and he always enjoyed it.

Still, the best sex for both of them was together, especially when Buzz turned Mickey on his belly and pushed into him, stretching him as far as he could. Mickey always had an orgasm when Buzz did that and Buzz always took great delight in doing it.

Early in their twentieth year together, Mickey noticed that Buzz was becoming moody and seemed to be losing his enthusiasm for things. After a few weeks of worrying about it, he called their doctor and made an appointment for a full physical for Buzz. Everything came back normal or negative, as appropriate, and Buzz was pronounced fit as any middle-aged man could be. That done, and still with no change in Buzz, Mickey decided to simply confront him with it.

He did what they always did when one or the other of them needed to talk: after work on Friday he stopped at a restaurant—this time Italian— and bought food to go. When Buzz came home there was gin in the freezer, the table was set and dinner was in the oven to stay warm. Buzz recognized the situation immediately.

"I need a shower first," he said, giving Mickey a kiss. "Then can we have martinis?"

Mickey kissed back. "Done. Go shower. And don't take the time to jerk off. I'll do it for you later."

Buzz brightened considerably and went to shower. He loved it when Mickey just took him in hand and jerked him off. It never took long and his orgasms were always wonderful.

They sat in the living room, in their comfortable chairs, Harry in Buzz's lap. They touched glasses and Buzz said, "Okay, what's this about?"

Mickey smiled. "For once it's about you. Buzz, what's going on? Why are you... I don't know, depressed is probably too strong a word, but you seem to have lost interest in things, in life."

Buzz sat quietly for a few moments before he said, "I am. I ... God damn it! I hate that firm, I hate my job, and I hate going to work in the morning." He sighed. "I guess I'm just having a mid-life crisis." Harry turned on his back and made a little sound, asking for attention. Buzz rubbed his belly.

"No you're not. If you were having a standard mid-life crisis you would have gone out and bought that red Porsche you keep looking at."

Buzz gave him a long look. "How do you know about the Porsche?"

Mickey laughed. "You aren't quite as subtle as you think you are, my sweet. When we go to Le Chat for dinner you always park so that we have to walk past the Porsche showroom. You see one on the street and you drool."

"I do not!"

"Well, almost. You have, shall I say, an unnatural interest in red Porsches. But that's not the point. The point is, you haven't gone out and bought one so this is not a simple mid-life crisis. So what is it?"

Buzz slumped in his chair. "Okay. It's childish I know, but I really do hate my job. I'm just not doing anything of any value, helping anyone or, as we love to say, pushing for justice. It's all corporate junk, arranging things so some guy can hustle more money from some company." He downed the last of his martini. "And I'm stuck in it. But there's no way out." He held out his glass. "Please?"

They talked for another hour and then ate dinner which wasn't as good as it would have been if it were fresh but they didn't notice. After dinner they took their wine back into the living room and sat together on the couch. Harry climbed up to his top floor condo and lay, quietly observing them and hugging his catnip mouse.

"You know, Buzz, why don't you go down to the Community Law Project and lawyer for them for a while? That might satisfy your need to, as you say, really do something."

Buzz laughed. "Can't. They don't pay anything."

"So?"

"So we have to live."

Mickey had a sudden flash of understanding. "Buzz? How much do you make?"

Buzz thought for a moment and then shrugged. "I don't know. You take care of all that stuff."

Mickey nodded. "Then I don't suppose you have even a clue what I make."

Again, Buzz shrugged. "No. Should I?"

"In this case it might have helped but no, in the long run it isn't really necessary. What is necessary is that you talk to me about this stuff." He refilled their wine glasses. "Look, if you want to go to work for the Community Law Project—or any other place for that matter—go do it. We'll get along. Get along very well."

"How?"

"Okay. Here's what you need to know. We live on my salary. We've been living on it for years. What you make, and you make a lot by the way, goes in the bank. We use some of it to pay for those cruises we both like so much and much of the rest goes into our investment account. What's left over just sits around at the bank."

"Really?" Buzz's face broke into a wide grin. "Is there enough for a red Porsche?"

Mickey laughed. "You idiot. You really want that red Porsche? We can go down tomorrow and you can write them a check for it." He leaned in and kissed Buzz. "But after that, you have to decide about your job."

"Monday. Right now we have to decide about something else. Is it going to be on your belly or on my back. Your choice."

It turned out to be both ways, Mickey on his stomach when they went to bed and Buzz on his back early in the morning.

They never did buy the red Porsche. Buzz did drive one once but found it to be more fun as a fantasy than as transportation. Buzz didn't quit his job, either. What he did do, however, was cut his time to two days a week and spend the other three at the Community Law Project, where he was able to do some very satisfying work. His law firm liked it too because they could tout their community service work. They did cut his salary but only in half and didn't reduce his yearly bonus at all.

But no life is all champagne and good sex and theirs wasn't either. Harry seemed to be getting listless and seemed to want fewer belly rubs but more body contact. He was constantly in one or the other of their laps and, though he purred, it wasn't as loud as it had been. They got worried and Buzz took him to his doctor.

When Mickey came home that afternoon he found Buzz on the couch. He had obviously been crying. Mickey didn't say a word but simply lifted Buzz's head, sat down and put his head in his lap. They stayed like that for a half hour before Buzz spoke.

"It was cancer," he said. "Everywhere. His insides were being eaten."

"Was he in pain?"

"Doctor Spike said no. He said this spread very fast in him and the pain would come soon but he didn't think it had yet. We made sure it wouldn't. I… I had him cremated." Buzz began to cry softly, tears running down his face and wetting Mickey's slacks. Mickey's tears fell on Buzz's shirt. They held on to each other.

After a while, and without a word, Buzz got up and went out to the kitchen. He returned with a damp towel and two icy martinis. He wiped Mickey's face with the towel and then his own. "We need this," he said, handing one of the martinis to Mickey. He held his own up and toasted the Kitty Condo. "To Harry and the joy he brought us."

They eventually acquired a new cat, this one called Harry2.

Then came February, 1998. It was very cold in San Francisco that month, with a lot of rain. One night Mickey, sitting close to the fireplace, said, "I've had it with this weather, Buzz. I got wet waiting for the bus this morning and I haven't dried out since. Then the dumb guys in New York call and want me to go out and walk around the building to make sure all the security cameras are working. Me, not the security guys. By the time I got finished I was soaked through my underwear."

Buzz laughed and handed him a martini. "Or would have been if you wore underwear."

Mickey took a sip of his drink. "That's not the point. Just because some store in Minneapolis gets ripped off because the security guys have jiggered the cameras is no reason to send me out in the rain. God, I wish it would warm up."

"Speaking of underwear, I had a client today who kicked her husband out because he refused to wear it."

"What? Was she a crazy person?"

Buzz drew himself up and crossed his arms over his chest. "I am a lawyer, sir, not a psychiatrist. I do not make those determinations." He laughed. "But between us, yeah, she was a crazy person. This was down in Palm Springs and his excuse was that none of the men there ever wear underwear. Her beef was that, around the house at least, he didn't wear much of anything and was always horny and often showed it. Outside he wore shorts that let his dick hang out when he stood a certain way which, I gather, he did a lot."

"Wow."

"Wow is right. I never did determine if it hung out of his shorts because the shorts were very short or because his dick was very long. Anyway, now he's suing her for alimony because she has a job and he doesn't. She, of course, doesn't want to pay."

"So why are they in San Francisco?"

"They aren't. She is. She had to get away from him and his hanging dick so she came here. Broke, of course."

By this time Mickey had had to put his drink on the floor because he was laughing so hard he was afraid he'd spill it.

"Hey, I'm not making this up. Really."

There was a short pause while the wheels turned in Mickey's head, just as Buzz had known they would.

"If nobody wears underwear in Palm Springs, it must be really warm there, right?"

Buzz smiled. "Yeah…"

"And if it's really warm there…"

Buzz interrupted. "Eighty-two degrees today. I checked."

"…then why are we here?"

Buzz laughed. "Because you haven't told your boss you're taking next week off. We're on a ten o'clock flight Friday morning."

Mickey got up and gathered Buzz into a hug. "How come you do great things like this?" He stepped back and looked Buzz up and down and then snapped his fingers. "I know! Because you want to have your way with me. Well, let me tell you something, mister." He kissed Buzz on the mouth. "Every day we're in Palm Springs, I'm yours to do with as you want, any time, anywhere. I'm that desperate. Oh, and did I mention that I love you?"

"You did. And I love you." He took Mickey's hand and put it on his crotch. "See?"

They ended up on the floor, rolling around in front of the fire and spilling Mickey's seed on the rug a couple of times."

Palm Springs turned out to be everything they wanted it to be. They rented a snappy little convertible at the airport and stayed at a clothing-optional gay resort called Some Guys. They'd never stayed at such a place before and found that they loved the freedom. They got right into the swing of things. The first afternoon they were there they went up on the sundeck and stood, side by side, holding hands, while a couple of guys gave them blow jobs. The guys turned out to be a couple, and Buzz and Mickey returned the favor the next morning.

They dressed and went out to eat the first night, and Buzz complained that they didn't have anything really suitable to wear. "My God, Mickey," Buzz complained, "I haven't worn shorts since I was a kid, much less owned a pair. And I want a pair of those sandals everyone has, they look so cool and comfortable." So they went shopping.

They were sent by Sam, one of the men at the front desk, to a department store called Lawton's. He said they had a fair selection and excellent prices, which turned out to be true. What they didn't have, Mickey observed, was style. Buzz didn't care, though, because they had exactly what he wanted.

Mickey bought two pairs of shorts and a tee shirt with "I Love Palm Springs" printed on it. When he was in the changing room trying on the shorts, Buzz came in and said, "Now make sure you don't hang out of those shorts. Not that anybody would divorce you if you did. In fact…" He reached for Mickey's crotch.

"Buzz, get out of here. Don't you know they have security cameras…" He was interrupted by a long kiss."

"Let 'em look at that," he said as he left, "and see if it doesn't make 'em stand up." Mickey could hear him laughing all the way back to the rack of shorts.

They had a wonderful week. Every restaurant they went to was good, the local people were friendly and they just felt closer to each other. They went to the weekly street fair on Thursday evening and found themselves walking down Palm Canyon Drive holding hands. Nobody did a double take, nobody scowled and a couple of guys winked at them. It was a very happy time.

The trouble with it was that when they got back to San Francisco the weather felt that much worse. Mickey began to plot.

The thing was, so did Buzz.

It took a while but one Friday night in August Mickey came home with pasta, two sauces, grilled sausages, an assortment of olives and a bottle of Chianti. When Buzz came home he immediately knew something was up.

He kissed Mickey and said, "Martinis first, then talk. What's…"

"Italian. Go shower."

Buzz grinned. "Do I have time to…" He made a fist and moved it up and down.

"Suit yourself," Mickey said. "Just remember, if you do you're going to be drinking a warm martini 'cause I'm pouring them now."

"Oh. Be right back."

He was, in record time. "So what are we doing?" he asked, settling on the couch.

"I want to talk about Palm Springs," Mickey said, sitting beside him.

Buzz grinned at him. "No you don't. You want to talk about moving to Palm Springs."

"How come I never get to have any secrets?"

"Because we've lived in each other's minds too long. Remember the red Porsche?"

Mickey laughed. "Okay, okay. I want to talk about moving to Palm Springs. Buzz, it's warm there and friendly. The City, for all its advantages, is crowded, the homeless are everywhere, they're all begging for money and the crazy ones stand around hurling insults at people. Palm Springs is... I don't know, it's quiet."

"Mickey, I'm hungry so let's just cut to the chase. How are we..." He looked at Mickey with narrowed eyes. "Of course! That store. Where we bought the shorts and sandals? You said it had no style so you've figured out a way to jazz it up. And make money doing it. Right? Enough to support us?"

Mickey nodded. "I think so. I've been doing some networking and investigating and got myself introduced to Mr. Lawton who just happens to own Lawton's Department Store in Palm Springs." He grinned. "Mr. Lawton also owns the shopping center around the store and that is giving him other problems to deal with. On top of that, his store manager quit not long ago and he is trying to do that, too. It isn't working."

"So it's a done deal?" Buzz finished his drink and held the glass out.

"Not quite," Mickey said, refilling the glass. "There's you to consider. You seem happy with the Law Project and tolerating the firm. So what do we do about..."

Buzz interrupted. "Can we live on what'll be coming in?"

"Oh, God yes. My salary will probably do it. If not, our investments generate quite a bit of cash as well."

Buzz took a sip of his drink. "I don't know where, all those years ago, you learned to make these things but you sure learned well. Anyway, let me tell you about my thinking over the past couple of months. See, I think I'd like to write a book, sort of a popular look at being a pro bono lawyer. I think I could do it and I think it would maybe sell." He laughed. "I also think it would be fun but you're not supposed to think that about work."

"I know. It really bugs them at the store that I really have fun managing it. Even with all the problems that come up."

"So anyway, if we move to Palm Springs perhaps I can get down to it and write my book."

Mickey laughed. "You'll be good at writing I'll bet. You really want to try it?"

He did.

They flew down to Palm Springs and hooked up with a real-estate guy named Victor. Victor didn't do much with rentals but he had a client who had just bought a condo but couldn't get away from Minneapolis for another ten months. He wanted to rent it out furnished and he'd allow pets. It was perfect for Buzz and Mickey. And Harry2.

Two weeks later they were officially Palm Springs residents.

TAYLOR CIRCLE

Things went well, as they often do in Palm Springs. Mickey, after a stressful week of suffocatingly close supervision by Mr. Lawton, convinced him that he did know what he was doing. Mr. Lawton, against his better judgment, gave him his head and tried to stay out of his way. He didn't always like what Mickey was doing but the results were clear on the next monthly sales report. Mr. Lawton went back to dealing with his shopping center full time and left Mickey alone.

Buzz bought himself a new computer and spent a couple of weeks learning how to use it. Writing wasn't quite as easy as he'd thought it would be but still, after three months he had what he considered to be a workable outline.

Towards the end of September they had a call from Victor, the real-estate guy, who told them his client wanted to take back his condo on November first. "I wanted to give you guys as much notice as I could," Victor said. "And if you've decided to stay in Palm Springs, I have a house I think you'll like."

Buzz and Mickey had already decided the move to Palm Springs was the best thing they'd done since that cold, foggy night in San Francisco twenty-three years ago so they went to see the house. At the same time, they put the San Francisco house on the market.

These things rarely work the way they're supposed to but this time they did. They loved the house Victor showed them on Taylor Circle and they thought the price was exceptionally good, so they bought it. At the same time their house in San Francisco became the object of a bidding war. The guys who finally won it wanted a short escrow so, with no planning on their part, their escrows closed on the same day. Even Victor was impressed.

Millie Jordan seemed a nice person and seemed anxious to get on with the sale. She offered Buzz and Mickey any of the furniture they wanted, telling them that what they didn't want would go to the Angel View Thrift Store, which, she explained, supported a very worthwhile charity.

"My daughter-in-law said I was to bring my bedroom furniture," she confided in them, "so I'll have something familiar around me. She's being so kind I didn't have the heart to tell her I really hate that furniture. The bed is too big and the drawers in that dresser haven't worked right since the day we bought it. But… what can I do?"

Mickey knew what she could do. "Look, Mrs. Jordan, we just got in something at the store that I think would be perfect for you. The bed is a queen, not as big as the king you have, and the rest of the pieces are well proportioned and rather stylish. Come down to the store when you can and have a look at it."

She did and she loved it. So Mickey arranged to have the manufacturer deliver an identical set to the daughter's house in Wichita. "Call your daughter-in-law up and explain to her that the guys who bought the house loved your bedroom furniture and begged you to leave it. You just couldn't turn them down so they bought you this stuff to replace it."

Millie looked at him a little wide-eyed. "They did?"

Mickey laughed. "They did. You don't have to tell her about the discount the store gives me."

And with that Buzz and Mickey became the second gay couple on Taylor Circle.

A couple of days after they moved in, an Angel View truck came to the house and took nearly all the furniture and leftover bric-a-brac away. Mickey looked at the empty space with a critical eye and smiled, thinking about how it would look when he got through with it.

The first neighbor to come calling was, of course, Brown, bearing one of Mrs. Brown's pecan pies. He was careful to refer to Buzz and Mickey as gay men in his welcome speech and they quickly came to like him and his no-nonsense honesty.

Next came the Sprakers, who brought a bottle of good wine for Buzz and Mickey and a small catnip mouse for Harry2. "I saw the carrier when you moved in and I couldn't wait to see her," Samantha said. "Is she adjusting to the new place?"

"Well," Buzz laughed, "first of all she's a he, Harry2 by name. And he's adjusting very well. He's being very thorough though so it'll take him a week or so to scope the place out. Then he'll be happy. And he's going to love that little mouse you brought. Catnip makes him crazy."

They went through the "Where is Mrs. Clark?" routine but when she got a "No, there isn't" she didn't bother to ask about a Mrs. O'Rourke. Mr. Spraker, again, didn't have a clue and said, "Well, we'd better be careful or Taylor Circle will get a reputation for being a bachelors' paradise."

Next came Wes and Bill from next door with a small bag of freshly made hard rolls. That they were freshly made impressed the hell out of Buzz. "Wow," he said, opening the bag and sniffing, "you made these?"

Wes looked up. "Yeah. Ever since he took those cooking classes we don't buy store bread anymore."

Buzz looked at Mickey, who shook his head. "Maybe when I retire."

They had cocktails in the living room, sitting on some chairs that even the thrift shop hadn't wanted. It wasn't long before Harry2 came sauntering in, looking for a likely lap. He chose Wes.

"Well, who have we here?" Wes asked, petting Harry2. Harry2 promptly turned on his back and presented his belly as a convenient place to rub.

"That's Harry2," Buzz said, "and he lives up to his name so if you don't want cat hair…"

Wes shook his head. "Like dog hair, cat hair just makes you well dressed." Harry2 began to purr. Wes laughed. "Noisy little guy, isn't he."

Buzz grinned. "You ought to hear him at six-thirty in the morning when he's sleeping on your pillow, six inches from your ear. He sounds like a vacuum cleaner."

"Speaking of vacuum cleaners," Mickey said, "do you guys have a house cleaner? We both hate cleaning the house and this place is quite a bit larger than the condo we just left."

Wes laughed. "Bill, bless his heart, does most of ours. He wouldn't let me do any of it when I was in college. He said learning was enough drudgery and I didn't need housework put on top of it. But if you guys find somebody, let us know. I think even Bill would be willing to let someone else do it now."

Buzz had a thought. "Hey, maybe someone in Prime Timers does housework. We ought to look through the newsletter, maybe they have an ad or something."

"What's Prime Timers?" Wes asked.

"A social club for older guys—you know, guys in their 'prime'— and their admirers," said Mickey. "It's fun. They get together for drinks in a different bar on Monday evenings and have dinners and lunches at various restaurants around town. You ought to look into it. We've met some nice guys there."

They decided that the next Monday Wes and Bill would join Mickey and Buzz and check the club out.

The neighborhood quickly absorbed Buzz and Mickey and it wasn't long before they felt like they'd lived there forever.

One Saturday morning in early March, Buzz said to Mickey, "Hey, you want a free breakfast?" He held up the newspaper. "The Green Palms Retirement Center will give us a free breakfast if we go tour the place."

Mickey laughed. "I don't think so. We're too young for a place like that. Let's go to the Rainbow Cactus instead. It won't be free but it does have all those hunky waiters."

"Yeah, and damn good Bloody Marys, too. You're on."

Across Taylor Circle the very same ad was read at Number 15. "George," Samantha said over her coffee, "it says here that that retirement place—you know, The Green Palms?— is giving couples a free breakfast if they go on a little tour to see the place."

George snorted. "Yeah, sure. Free. You get a bad cup of coffee and a stale Danish and then they put the pressure on you. These things are all the same: they want to separate you from your wallet."

"I don't know," Samantha said. "My friend Janice has eaten there and says they have really good food. Come on, it can't hurt and it might be fun."

So George, sensing that if he didn't he would never hear the end of it, called for a reservation.

On Sunday, when they arrived, even George couldn't help but be impressed. First of all, the place was immaculate, even the landscaping. Second, the dining room was light, airy and very welcoming. Third, and the clincher, was that they offered eggs Benedict on the menu. George loved eggs Benedict and Samantha couldn't poach an egg to save her soul.

They started with a plate of mixed fruit which proved to be wonderfully fresh and sweet. Samantha followed that with a crab salad dressed with a lovely basil vinaigrette. George's eggs Benedict were, to George's taste, perfect—and they looked pretty, too.

After breakfast a handsome young man came over to the table and, calling them by name, introduced himself as Duane. He would be the one to show them around the place and answer any questions they might have. The first thing George had to say was, "I suppose you only have eggs Benedict on the menu when you're promoting the place."

Duane laughed. "You know, Mr. Spraker, people often think that. But no, everything you saw on the menu this morning is on the menu every morning. We don't have to put special things on to promote Green Palms because what we always have is always special."

George nodded and grumbled something unintelligible.

For Samantha, the best thing—besides the fact that she would only have to cook if she really wanted to—was the little bus that took residents to various shopping malls around the area on a regular schedule. Since she didn't drive, and since George hated shopping, this clinched the deal for her, the same way the eggs Benedict clinched it for George.

Almost as an afterthought, they looked at the apartments. All of them were nice and any one of them would suit the Sprakers perfectly. They left with a couple of floor plans, "to think about it." They both knew they were going to buy one of the apartments but George didn't want to look too eager. They shouldn't have bothered. Duane had already reserved one of the apartments for them.

So, in March of 1999, Number Fifteen Taylor Circle went on the market. It sold in five weeks to a retired couple named George McGuire & Michael Williams.

CHAPTER THREE

GEORGE & MICHAEL

George and Michael first met in 1967 at a Welcome Back Faculty party thrown by George's wife, Irene. Irene had ambitions to be the "First Lady of the College" and this party was part of her campaign to get George appointed president of the college. George went along with it, partly because he thought it might be fun to be president of the college but mainly because it was all financed by Irene's father. In fact, everything about her was financed by her father—who could well afford it. He'd been CFO at a very large and influential bank before he retired and, now that his wife was gone, his daughter had become his main diversion in life. George was fairly comfortable with this arrangement since it took a lot of pressure off of him and his professor's salary.

Irene and George had two children, a daughter named Melinda and a son named Troy. Melinda was thirteen and deep in the throes of adolescence while Troy was twelve and just beginning to pick his way through puberty. Melinda was going to grow up to be a copy of her mother, tall, with thick, golden hair and, George was afraid, her selfsame need to be somebody. Troy was quite a different child, he was easy going, tolerant and always saw the quirky side of life. He was fun to be around.

This afternoon Melinda was helping her mother serve cocktails and introducing herself to everyone, especially the ones who looked like they might be important. Troy, on the other hand, was hiding in his bedroom, playing with himself, trying out this funny jack-off—or jerk-off, he wasn't sure which was correct—thing the boys down the street were always talking about. In retrospect, he probably had more fun that afternoon than everyone else in the house combined.

"Oh, Daddy, have you met Mr. Williams?" Melinda asked, handing George a glass of white wine and offering another to Michael.

"I don't think so." He shook Michael's hand. "But the name is familiar."

Michael smiled. "Maybe you noticed it on your office assignment sheet. I'm Michael Williams, your soon to be office mate."

George laughed. "Of course. From Chicago, I think?"

"A little suburb of. Small college no one's ever heard of."

"Can't be any smaller than this one. Welcome to Doane College, Michael." He'd picked up on Michael's wedding ring early in the conversation. "Your wife here?"

Michael pointed. "Yes, she's over there, talking with that pretty woman who, I gather, is your wife."

Melinda tapped her dad on the arm. "The Dean just came in, Daddy. I think…"

"Oh, yes, of course." He turned to Michael. "Drink up and let's meet the Dean." He took Michael's elbow and steered him across the room.

In front of the fireplace, Joanne, Michael's wife, had about finished sizing up Irene and decided they probably wouldn't be friends. Irene was a social climber and Joanne had no time for people like that. Besides, what was to climb? In a town of eleven thousand the only society was at the college and Joanne had no time for that, her husband notwithstanding. Joanne was a nurse and she actually had a job, unlike most of the women she had met so far. She had just been hired as the head nurse in the local hospital's Intensive Care Unit and was proud of it. She also didn't suffer fools gladly.

Michael, on the other hand, was easy-going, cut others a lot of slack and thought life was pretty good although he wasn't sure about living in a small town. He'd been accustomed to being able to escape to Chicago now and again.

Michael and Joanne had two boys, Jack who was eight and Sam who was seven. The boys were, on the whole, quite well behaved and were the light of Michael's eyes.

When she'd had enough Joanne caught Michael's eye and he gave a slight nod. They met near the door, said good evening to George and Irene and made good their escape.

"Do you suppose these things happen often?" Joanne asked on the way home. "I don't know how many of them I can take."

Michael laughed. "Hey, you can always say you have to work."

She sighed. "Well, I hope you don't expect me to become chummy with your office mate's wife. She's already tried to get me to join some damn committee or other."

"Hey, you'd be good. You could whip those women into shape at the first meeting."

"Well, I'm not going to. I hate college politics!"

He reached out and patted her hand. "Don't worry about it, honey. You don't have to. I'll handle it for both of us."

Things went along very well for the next seven or so years. Joanne and Irene didn't see each other more than absolutely necessary and Michael and George found that they were quite compatible as office mates.

Both George and Michael, separately, managed to get away to Lincoln once in a while and, less often, to Columbus in order to satisfy their "other" needs. Neither, of course, knew about the other. In a small college town, a man, especially if he is married and has children, doesn't advertise that sort of thing.

All in all, it was The Good Life in Small College Town America.

Or it was until 1977.

On a blustery Monday morning in October, George came into the office early, carrying two cups of Starbuck's coffee. Handing one cup to Michael, he said, "I suppose I'd better tell you first. Irene and I are getting a divorce."

Michael almost dropped his coffee. "You?" He put his coffee down and stood, putting his hand on George's shoulder. "Is there anything I can do?"

George shook his head. "It's okay. I mean, we're still friends and all. And her father is okay with it, that's the important thing."

Michael felt genuine pain. "Yeah, but are you okay?"

"I suppose." He gave a rueful laugh. "I never would have made president anyway so…"

Michael sat down. "Do the kids know?"

"No, not yet. Irene wants to handle that and they're at college so she's going to wait a day or two and she and her father will go out to see them." He shrugged. "Sort of tell them in person. It'll probably be okay. I mean, she's twenty-three and he's twenty-one." He laughed. "I guess it'll give him an excuse to go out and get drunk or something." He eyed Michael. "You are the best kind of friend, Michael."

"Huh?"

"You haven't asked the classic 'what happened' question."

Michael shook his head. "I know you pretty well, George. Well enough to know it wasn't just one thing. It was lots of them and you probably haven't sorted them all out yet. And," he smiled, "you may not want to share some of them. There are some things you don't share with anyone you're not sleeping with."

George broke into a long and loud laugh. Michael wasn't sure what was funny but laughed along with him. For George it was his first real laugh in three days.

So George called a lawyer, found a small, one bedroom apartment, argued with Irene over the furniture he wanted to take, and that was that.

It wasn't nearly so easy for Michael.

It happened in June of 1978. Michael came home to find Joanne there, even though she was supposed to be working a late shift that day. She was in the kitchen, drinking gin on the rocks.

"Who is Jeffery?"

He thought for a moment. "Jeffery? I don't think... One of my students maybe?"

"Jeffery Carns." At his blank look she went on. "Tall, reddish blond hair? You had coffee with him this afternoon." Her voice grew brittle. "At a time you told me you'd be in an urgent meeting with the dean."

He was nearly speechless. "I had..."

She slammed her drink down on the counter, scattering ice and gin. "Get off it, Michael. You were seen in the company of an Emergency Room nurse named Jeffery Carns, the most flagrant, most notorious homosexual in the hospital." There was a long pause, then: "Well? I'm waiting. And while I'm waiting perhaps you can think up some lie to explain away those trips to Lincoln. I often wondered why you had to go up there to do research when the library here is ten times better." Another pause. "Well?"

"Where are the boys?"

"Over at Mary and Joe's, having a sleepover." She took a gulp of the gin left in her glass. "So what do you have to say for yourself or do I have to spell it out?"

Michael took her glass from her and filled it, along with another for himself, with ice. And gin. When he handed it to her he said in a quiet voice, "It's not as bad as you make it out to be. It's bad but…"

"You're damn right it's bad," she yelled at him. "You're a faggot! A God damn faggot! Well, I can't live with a faggot, not anymore." Her voice turned ugly. "I'll bet you take it up the ass, don't you, Michael. The bigger the better, right? Is that what you do with Jeffery? Take that big ole dick of his up your ass?" She took another gulp of her gin. "Well, I just hope it hurts when he shoves it up there. Hurts like hell."

"Joanne, please…"

She raised her voice to just below a scream. "Get out! Now. Out of my sight, out of my house." Her voice dropped to a growl. "Go!"

Michael put down his glass and picked up his keys. When he turned to the back door she very quietly said, "And if I ever find out that you ever laid a hand on either one of my boys I will kill you. As God is my witness, I will kill you."

When he turned back to her she was holding a knife and he knew she would not hesitate to use it.

"That, I have never done, never even thought… Goodbye Joanne."

In the car, once he was away from the house, he realized that he had no idea what to do or where to go. He drove aimlessly around for a while, trying not to think, until it occurred to him that what he needed to do was to die. The more he thought about it the better an idea it seemed. He wouldn't ever have to face anyone who might know, he wouldn't have to try to explain anything to Jack and Sam and best of all, the pain would go away. Yes, death seemed the obvious solution.

But in the end he knew he couldn't do that to Jack and Sam. Joanne could take care of herself but the boys, eighteen and nineteen, he couldn't dump on them. So he went to a hotel, took a hot bath and went to bed. He didn't sleep, couldn't slow his mind down, but staring at the ceiling, kept the worst of the images at bay.

At six o'clock he got up, showered, dressed in yesterday's clothes and went to the office. There wasn't anything else to do. On an impulse he stopped at Starbucks and bought two coffees.

"What the hell happened to you?" George said when Michael walked in. "You look like… Well, you don't look good."

Michael handed him a coffee. "We had a fight," he said. "Joanne threw… uh, asked me to leave. I spent the night in a hotel."

"You idiot. You should have come to me. You could have slept on my couch. Remember that if… well, if you ever need a place to stay. Now, what are you going to do?"

"I truly don't know, George. I can't think."

George sat down and looked at him. Softly he said, "Well, I can. The first thing you need to do is talk to someone." He held up the palm of his hand. "Not me! You need to talk to someone who can help you. Look, when Irene and I were having so much trouble I spent a lot of time talking to a guy who helped me figure out what to do. Dr. Miller. He's a therapist and a damn good one. If I can get him to see you will you go talk to him?"

Michael nodded. He just wanted someone to tell him what to do. So he didn't have to think. Thinking seemed to him to be dangerous.

George got on the phone immediately. Michael didn't listen, he just drank his coffee and tried to make his mind a blank, block out the sound of Joanne's voice calling him a faggot.

"Okay," George said, hanging up the phone. He'll see you at nine, as a favor to me. Here's his address." He wrote something on a piece of paper and handed it to Michael. "I've got to get to my class. Will you be all right until then?"

Michael nodded and shrugged. "Yeah. Don't worry about me."

"I'll worry about you if I want to." He patted Michael on the shoulder. " Be careful." He picked up his briefcase and went out the door.

Michael sat in the silent office for an hour and then went to Dr. Miller's office. He was a half hour early, but the receptionist showed him into the doctor's office immediately.

Michael spent nearly two hours with Dr. Miller and came out of his office a far more calm and thinking man than he'd been when he went in. The receptionist had him fill out some papers and he wrote a check for the best two-hundred dollars he had ever spent. He also made an appointment for the next week.

Back at his office George took one look at him and said, "You liked him, didn't you?"

Michael nodded. "He helped me shut off the emotion so I could think. Yeah, he was wonderful. I see him again next week."

"Good. Look, if you need a place to stay tonight, mine's available. You'll be stuck on the couch but it's pretty comfortable. I should know, I slept on it enough nights."

"Okay, thanks George. I…" His phone rang and he picked it up. It was his son, Jack.

"Dad? What's going on, Dad? Mom said you… well, you weren't coming home anymore. She said… well, that you…"

He could tell from Jack's voice that there was more. "It's okay, Jack. You can tell me what she said."

"She said you could tell us why, and if you didn't she would. Dad? What did she mean by that?"

"I guess she meant that we see things differently and she's going to give me the opportunity to tell you my side. That was very kind of her and I'll tell her so. Where are you? And where is your brother?"

There was a long pause, then, in a puzzled voice, "Home. But she said you can't come here. What…"

"Listen, it's a nice day and I'll bet it would be okay with her if I just came up on the front porch. How about that?" He looked at his desk clock. "I tell you what. I'll pick up a couple of pizzas and we can have lunch on the front porch while we talk. How's that sound?"

"O… okay. Be sure to get one with anchovies. Sam loves anchovies. Everything on mine."

Michael laughed for the very first time that morning. A teenaged boy's brain may be confused and need to talk but his stomach is still running the show. "I won't forget. I'll see you in a half, three quarters of an hour."

"Okay, Dad. We'll wait on the front porch."

As he left the office George looked up and grinned. "See? Life isn't over. Have a good lunch and if I don't see you this evening I'll figure you managed to win her over. But in case you don't, here's a key to my place. After you talk to the boys you might want a shower and a nap."

He took the key. "The chance of my winning her over, as you say, is exactly zero so I'll see you tonight. And thanks again. For everything, especially Dr. Miller."

He stopped at the local pizza parlor, the one the college kids said was the best. Just walking in started him salivating and he realized he was very hungry. He ordered three large pizzas to go, with everything, anchovies on one, and three Cokes.

The boys were delighted. They had set up a card table and some folding chairs, gotten napkins, plates and glasses and Sam had even found a little vase and had put a couple of flowers in it for the center of the table.

While they ate they talked about summer plans and what would happen in the fall when Sam started college. Both he and Jack had decided not to go to Doane College and were all set to go to a small school near Chicago, the one where Michael had taught before coming to Nebraska.

When the pizzas had been demolished and the Cokes finished, Michael started talking. "What has happened between your mother and me is because of me. When I was a boy, younger than you guys, I made a discovery. I found that I was attracted to other boys. You have to remember, in those days there was little understanding of those things and what understanding there was, was hidden."

Jack blurted out, "You were queer?" There was a pause while Jack thought about it. "How did you know?"

Michael sighed. He'd hoped he wouldn't have to get into this, at least not this soon. But the tone of Jack's voice told him Jack was worried—worried about himself, probably worried that this thing might have somehow infected him, too. "Well, the first thing I knew was that when I masturbated, you know, jacked-off, I thought about boys, not girls, always. The second thing was, there were a couple of guys at school that I… that I played with."

"You mean that you had sex with?" Sam this time.

"Yes, that I had sex with. The trouble was, with each of them it wasn't very long before they discovered girls and lost interest in me." He bowed his head. "Look guys, I know this is hard to hear and brings up a lot of questions in your minds. I saw a doctor this morning, a therapist, who helped me a lot. He said he'd be happy to talk with either one of you if you want, maybe help you figure out what's going on here." He pulled two cards out of his pocket and handed one to each of the boys, "Take these, call him any time. It'll be completely confidential and no one will know. I'll pay for it of course but he won't tell me who came to see him or how many times. Okay? Please."

Both boys looked at the cards and put them in their wallets. Then Jack looked up at him. "So if you were queer, why did you marry Mom?"

Michael picked up his Coke but the glass was empty. His mouth was dry. "You know? I'd much rather be called gay than queer but if you can't, I'll understand." He put his glass back on the table. "Why did I marry your mother? The main reason was that I fell in love with her. I still love her today. I also wanted you guys. Well, I didn't know that what I wanted would turn out to be you guys but I wanted children, wanted to be a dad." He took a deep breath, to get the catch out of his voice. "And I got the best two reasons in the world for being a dad."

Sam spoke up. "I didn't think quee… uh, gays fell in love. At least not with women."

"Thank you Sam. I appreciate that." He smiled at Sam and thought *The kid is really trying.* He said, "Well the real trouble is, you can't control who you fall in love with and you can't control your basic nature. Your mom and I were married for a long time before I finally gave in to my need for…" How do you explain something like this to your sons? He shook his head. "Oh, hell, to my need for a man. There, I've said it. Sometimes I need a man. It's my nature."

Jack laughed. "Boy, I can't wait to hear Mom's take on this."

Michael smiled. "It'll be different from mine, I'm sure of that. Oh, and Sam? Gays do fall in love."

"I know. It's just better if they fall in love with each other. So what are you going to do now?"

"Nothing, really. I'm going to stay away from your mom for a while, teach my classes," he shrugged, "worry about you."

Jack got up and went around the table to his father and hugged him. "Don't worry about us, Dad. We'll be okay. Really."

Michael didn't care if his son did see the tears running down his cheeks. "Thank you, Jack." He looked up. "Thank you, Sam. Thank you both with all my heart." It took some effort but he managed to pull himself together.

"When Mom gets… I don't know, used to this I guess, will you come and have dinner with us?"

"Of course I will, Sam. And we'll still do stuff together, I'm not leaving your lives. It's just… well, I probably won't be living here for a while." He could see that neither of the boys thought he'd ever be living there again. He didn't actually think he would either. "Now, if you would let me in the house, I need to get some clothes to wear."

He saw conflict in the faces of both boys. Finally Jack spoke up, "We can't, Dad. We promised Mom."

"She changed the locks, too," Sam said. "Yesterday."

"Shit," Michael said under his breath.

"But she left those for you." Sam pointed at a couple of suitcases that he hadn't noticed behind the swing.

"Well, that was very thoughtful of her," he said, hoping the sarcasm didn't show. "Oh, and give her this," he handed Jack another of Dr. Miller's cards. "Same deal. No one knows, I pay. Okay?"

"Okay. Hey, where will you be? How can we get hold of you?"

"You'll have to call me at the office. I'm going to stay with Dr. McGuire for a few days, I guess. He got divorced a few months ago so we can commiserate with each other."

Sam looked at him sharply. "Is he qu… gay too?"

Michael laughed. "I never asked him but no, I don't think so. And Sam? I know this is hard for you both and I want both of you to know how much I appreciate the effort you're making."

Jack then said something Michael never would have expected from a nineteen-year-old: "You do stuff like that. When you love your dad."

Michael thought he might cry again.

They had a group hug and by the time Michael went down the stairs with his two suitcases, all of them had tears in their eyes.

Michael took George's advice and went to his place, had a long shower and stretched out on the couch. He was asleep within minutes.

When George came home he fixed drinks for them and showed Michael around the place so he could find things. "I don't suppose you're going to be here all that long but you might as well make yourself comfortable."

He was wrong about the time, right about the comfort.

The days and weeks moved along. Joanne was adamant about not letting Michael back in the house but did allow him to take the rest of his clothes. He knew that somebody did go to see Dr. Miller because he got a bill for six-hundred dollars. He thought it was probably worth it. He had two more sessions with Dr. Miller himself and knew they were worth the money.

He found that living with George was quite comfortable, the couch not withstanding. They ate out a lot and when they ate in Michael usually cooked. George turned out to actually like doing the laundry so Michael always had clean socks, shirts and underwear.

But it was lonely. When you're accustomed to living with someone, intimately, sleeping with them, sleeping alone on a couch, no matter how comfortable, feels wrong.

One night, after Michael had been on George's couch for three weeks, Michael started thinking about his life and how he was living it and was suddenly overwhelmed with an emotion akin to grief. He could hardly breathe and was being taken over by a feeling of hopelessness and, in the background, panic. He struggled with it as long as he could but finally he gave in to it. He got out of bed and went into George's room.

"I'm scared," he said with a quiver in his voice. "Please George? Please, could I..."

George put his book down on the nightstand and looked up at Michael. "Of course," he said, lifting the covers and moving over slightly. "Here, where it's warm."

Michael got into the bed, next to George. He was shaking and George put his arm under his neck and pulled him close. "It's okay, Michael. It'll pass." He hugged him. "You're safe here with me."

They stayed that way for a few minutes, George holding Michael, both of them staring at the ceiling. Then George leaned over Michael, kissed him briefly on the mouth and turned out the light. "Go to sleep, Michael," he said, turning Michael on his side and wrapping his arms around him. He pressed himself against Michael's back and petted Michael's belly, much as one would comfort a baby. "I'm here, Michael."

Michael did, in fact, go to sleep, almost immediately. It took George a little longer.

Somewhere around three George awakened to find Michael pressing back against him. He was hard and Michael had moved around so George's erection lay in the crack between the cheeks of his ass. George involuntarily gave Michael a couple of humps and Michael pressed back each time.

"You want this, Mikey? You want it to happen?"

He barely heard Michael's whispered "Yes."

George fumbled in the nightstand, trying not to move away from Michael. He found what he wanted and uncapped the tube with one hand. Then he moved slightly so he could spread a thick coat of the jelly on his now aching dick. He moved again, so the head of his dick was positioned against Michael's sphincter. Then he waited.

He didn't wait long. Michael slowly pushed back, taking all of George into him, all in one slow movement. When he settled into George's coarse hair he let out a long sigh as he felt the fear and pain of the past weeks drain out of him, to be replaced with George and the pleasure he brought.

George went slowly but it still didn't last long. Neither of them had had sex with anyone but themselves since Michael had come to stay and even that hadn't happened very often for either one of them. While he was coming George took hold of Michael and that was all it took to push Michael over the brink as well.

Afterward, nothing was said until George went to withdraw. Then Michael spoke very quietly. "Don't. Please? Just stay."

George pushed himself completely in again. "Okay, Mikey. I'll stay until you need me out."

Michael sighed and George thought he had gone to sleep until he squeezed down on George a couple of times. "If you don't stop that, Mikey, you'll get me started again," George whispered. Michael didn't stop.

The second time took longer than the first and brought both of them more pleasure. George stroked Michael's dick in the same rhythm as he was stroking into him. Even when Michael came, he kept up the same rhythm, which made Michael come again. Each time Michael came George thought he should stop and let him rest but Michael was having none of it. If George paused Michael pushed back on him, asking for more and George was always happy to give him more.

After George came, and Michael came for the third time, they slept. George went soft and slowly slipped out of Michael but a couple of hours later, when they woke, he was hard again and he pushed easily back in. "Is it okay Mikey? You're not sore, are you?"

Michael squeezed down on George a couple of times and then chuckled.

"What's funny?"

"Nothing's funny. It's happy."

George thought for a moment before he said, "Yeah, it is, isn't it?"

They moved around the bed, trying out new positions, and laughing and kissing and touching each other everywhere. They spent a lot of time at it, holding back, pushing further up the mountain of pleasure until they couldn't hold it anymore and had to let go. It was always a very explosive letting go.

When they finally disconnected they took a shower together, dressed and went out for breakfast. Both of them were surprised to find that breakfast was long gone; it was after lunchtime. They ate burgers with bacon and Swiss cheese and onions. "It's okay as long as we both have onions," George said with a grin. "That way you can't tell if it's you or me you're tasting."

After lunch they walked around the big park and talked.

"She found out?" George asked, tossing a pebble into the lake.

"Yeah." He smiled for the first time in a long time. "She didn't understand. Any of it."

"Me too. But ours was easier. She insisted that we go to counseling. I went to Dr. Miller and she went to his wife. They helped us keep our heads." He laughed. "Don't get me wrong, we did our share of screaming at each other, but even there, the venom was minimized." He picked up another pebble. "How'd she find out?"

Michael chuckled. "One of her friends saw me with a guy. We were only having coffee but she knew that he's gay and made assumptions. She offered those assumptions to Joanne."

"Well, wouldn't her assumptions have been true at some point? I mean…"

"No. He and I… We do the same thing so it wouldn't have worked. Neither of us even wanted to try."

George stopped and looked at Michael. "Is that, uh, is that all you do? What we did last night?"

Michael took the pebble out of George's hand. "Mostly. I… Well, I just never developed a knack for the other." He skipped the pebble over the lake surface and then turned to look at George. "Besides, I like what I do. Being the receiver, I mean. It makes me feel, well, feel like I'm part of the man, I guess. So…"

George laughed.

"What's funny?"

"You. Me. Us. I'm exactly the same as you are only I'm the giver. But you know what? When I'm inside a man, it makes me feel like he's a part of me. He's given himself to me, trusted himself to me. He's mine, at least for the time I'm inside him and, for that time, I need to take care of him, make him safe. And, of course, bring him pleasure." He looked at Michael. "Does that make any sense?"

Michael grinned. "Of course it does. It's what you did last night. You took care of me, you made me feel safe, and you brought me great pleasure. I only hope I did the same for you. At least the pleasure part."

"You did. Oh, my God you did." He looked around and then quickly kissed Michael on the mouth. "Let's go home."

They did, and spent the afternoon in bed. There they learned more and more about their compatibility. They learned that they both liked the feel of a man in their mouths, they both liked the taste of a man when he came and they both liked to kiss. They learned that neither of them really liked the classic "69" position. "I can't concentrate properly," George said. "When I'm in a man's mouth I want to feel what he's doing, let him move me along at his own pace. I don't want to worry about him, how he's doing, where he is. I suppose it's kind of selfish but it's the way I am."

"I can do it," Michael answered, "but it's never as pleasurable as it is thinking about only one thing. Some guys lose interest after they've come so I nearly always go first, let him do me and then I do him. It's funny about me, though. I'm often more horny after I've had an orgasm than I was before. Isn't that weird?"

George crawled up from between Michael's legs and laid his weight on him, covering him, their erections nestled against each other. "There is nothing weird about you, Mikey, except maybe that we're so in tune with each other. I wish I'd met you when I was in my teens, just starting out. We'd still be together you know."

Michael kissed him and quietly said, "I know. I feel it. But it's okay. We still have a lot of time."

About five months later, George came in from the mailboxes one evening, holding a letter.

"Who's it from?" Michael asked, handing him a drink.

"Odd. It's from Melinda. She's never written to me before in her life." He tore the envelope open and took out a neatly written card. He read it, said, "You bitch," and read it again, his face getting more and more red.

"What?"

He tore the card into eight or nine pieces and looked up at Michael. "Well, it seems that my daughter is going to get married. To some sort of fundamentalist sect leader, I gather. She has invited me to the wedding on the condition that I not bring you with me. You, it seems, have led me into sins too abominable to name and the likes of you are not welcomed by her, her husband-to-be or their church." He laughed, but it wasn't pretty. "By extension, neither am I welcome, I'd say." He took a large swallow of his drink and said, "I wonder how long it will take her to grow out of this?"

Michael kneeled down and put his arms around George. "You may go, you know," he said quietly. "I can stay home. Or, if you want, I can just wait in the car."

George kissed him, a very tender kiss. "Thank you, Michael. It's for reasons like that that I love you. But no, I think she—and I—will be better off if I don't go." He held up his glass. "May I have another?"

A week later there was a phone call from Irene, George's ex-wife. She wanted to know why he hadn't responded to Melinda's invitation.

"Oh, is that what it was? An invitation? It read like an indictment."

Irene tried to smooth things over but George was not going to be smoothed and she ended the conversation by hanging up on him.

A couple of days after that his son Troy called: "Hi, Dad. How's it going?" After some small talk, including Troy asking after Michael, they got down to the reason for the call. "You know, Dad, you really should rethink this wedding thing. I know, I know. Melinda isn't the most diplomatic person in the world but she's torn between that guy and her family. I know she wants you there, she told me so. She's very unhappy you turned the invitation down."

"I didn't turn it down. I tore it into small pieces and fed them to the fire. It seemed the place for it."

"Oh, come on, Dad. You know what I mean. Listen, would you come if I got her to invite Dr. Williams, too? Maybe as your guest or something?"

George actually laughed. For the first time, he could actually laugh about this. "Oh, Troy, someday you should listen to what you just said. I guess it'll come as a surprise to you, and maybe the rest of them, too, to hear this but Michael and I are not guests or friends or acquaintances. We are, in every sense of the word, a unit. We live together, we eat together, we sleep together. And yes, we do that, too, whatever it is that you're thinking. So no, it would not help if she invited Dr. Williams also. The bridge is burned until she elects to un-burn it."

"But Dad…"

"Ask her sometime what she said to me in her little note. The contents of her mind might surprise you—or perhaps horrify you. Her view of Dr. Williams might also. I'm going to hang up now, before this goes any further. Call me again, when we can talk about something pleasant. Better yet, come over and have a drink with us, maybe dinner. Michael is a great cook." He hung up.

A month after that, over dinner, Michael said, "How closely are you tied to this place? I mean the college, the town and," he shrugged, "maybe even the people."

George thought for a moment. "Not very. I like the college and most of the other teaching staff. Some in Administration I could happily strangle but overall, it's okay. Why?"

"Well, there's a former student of mine who is now an administrator at Santa Fe college in New Mexico. He's a nice guy and came out to me one day, out of the blue. He'd decided that he couldn't live in his closet any longer and was slowly coming out to his teachers and fellow students. Anyway, I had a call from him…"

"This isn't Jeremy Hutchison, is it?"

"As a matter of fact, it is. You knew him?"

George laughed. "Everyone knew him. Brave thing he did. At first I thought he was coming on to me but no such luck. You?"

Michael laughed. "We are alike, aren't we? Yeah, I thought the same thing but he wasn't, more's the pity."

"So, you had a call from him?"

"Yeah. It seems that we aren't as far under the radar as we thought. Someone, a student I gather, wrote to him and told him that we, you and I, are suddenly living together, without our wives. That information prompted Jeremy to call this morning, probing not too delicately to find out if we're a couple. When I told him we are, he wondered if we would consider relocating to New Mexico."

"What? Why would... wait a minute, you mean he's offering us jobs? At this college... whatever it is?"

"That's it. He says that things are quite a bit more friendly in Santa Fe and he thinks we would, as he put it, thrive there."

George looked up at him. "How... How tied are you to this place?"

Michael thought for a long time before he said, "Like you: not very." There was a long pause while each of them mulled things over in their minds. "It'd be nice," Michael said, "not to worry about it, not to always be aware of what people are thinking—or worse yet, what I think they're thinking."

George got up, walked around the table and hugged Michael. "We are alike, aren't we?"

So they flew out to Santa Fe and spent a few days with Jeremy Hutchison and his partner, an older man named Adolph, who obviously doted on him. They toured the campus and the town and thought they could happily live and work there. They met the president of the college over dinner at Jeremy and Adolph's and, in the end, they returned to Nebraska with new jobs and new friends. It was a very successful trip.

The move to Santa Fe was easy since George had rented the apartment furnished and neither one of them had taken much from their former homes—or lives for that matter. In Santa Fe they bought a small cottage and started on the road to furnishing a home and starting a life, a life together and a life out of the closet. It felt good to both of them.

Six months or so after they moved to Santa Fe Michael had a letter from his son Jack asking if he could come and visit them. He also asked if he could bring a friend. Of course the answer to both was 'yes.'

They drove to Albuquerque together to meet Jack's plane and were both pleasantly surprised when Jack's 'friend' turned out to be a young lady named Claire. Michael was introduced to her as 'Dad' and George as an awkward pause.

"Damned if I know what to call you, Sir," Jack said. "Dr. McGuire seems a little formal but George doesn't seem very respectful. What..."

"Call him Pop, why don't you?" Claire broke in. "He looks like a man who would be called Pop. Anyway that's what I'm going to call him." She turned to George. "Okay, Pop?"

George threw back his head and laughed. "I think that would be wonderful, Claire." He turned to Jack. "I knew whoever you brought with you would turn out to be our kind of people. Good show, Jack."

Jack hugged him. "Thanks, Pop." Then he hugged his father. "You got a good one, Dad. Keep him."

They spent the afternoon getting acquainted and in the evening went out for dinner. Jack insisted on paying for dinner which made his father proud. Later, there was no awkwardness about Jack and Claire sharing a room and bed. Jack had said that they had been living together for a couple of months so it wasn't altogether a surprise.

The next day George offered to show Claire around a few of the galleries in town and everybody understood that was meant to give Michael and Jack some time alone to catch up with each other.

The first topic, of course, was Claire. "She's a nice person," Michael said, "we're glad you brought her. You... uh, you have plans?"

Jack laughed. "It's that obvious, huh? Well, I, that is, we, do. We're going to get married. I just wanted you to meet her before I sprung it on you."

"Us to meet her or her to meet us?"

"Oh come on, Dad, it's not like that. She doesn't have any problem with guys like you and Dr. Mc... uh, Pop. I told her about you and she's cool with it. She has an uncle or somebody who's, you know, who's gay. He's still part of the family."

Michael tapped his beer bottle against Jack's in a small salute. "You know? You turned out better than I had any right to expect. I worried a little."

"What about, Dad?"

"Oh, silly things, mostly. Like would you hate me because of the way I am. And would you think maybe some of... of me had rubbed off on you. Or Sam. You know..."

Jack laughed. "I guess we did think about that. But Jesus, Dad, what you guys do... I mean, I can do it just as well with my hand, maybe even better sometimes. So..."

Michael shook his head. "And you know this, how?"

"Well, after that afternoon when you told us about you... well, we did think maybe we could somehow inherit it or something. So we tried it out for a while, just to see."

"You and Sam? You... You had sex? With each other?"

"Yeah, for a couple of weeks. We figured it was the only way to know if, well, if we were that way. Like I said, it was okay but it sure didn't have the kick it does with a woman." He drank his beer for a moment. "Then Sam decided that might be because we were brothers so we got one of his gay friends to do it with us."

Michael was stunned by this—but he couldn't let Jack know that—so he said the first thing that came into his mind. "A three-way? How did that go?"

"Pretty much the same. He's smaller than Sam so that part felt better but all in all it was pretty much a bust. Like I said, I can do better with my hand." He grinned. "But I did learn one thing: Sam is a great kisser."

Michael was silent while he processed this information. When he realized that Jack was staring at him he smiled and said, "Sorry, son. It's just that I never imagined you guys were that creative. To go and try it out. Most guys wouldn't have the guts to do that. They'd just worry about it and get all tied up inside." He finished his beer. "And Sam feels the same way?"

"Pretty much. He's living with his girlfriend. He says she doesn't want to get married until they decide to have a kid. Personally I think they should just go ahead and do it. Which brings me back to my original point. What do you think of Claire?"

"Well, I think maybe she just might be the perfect woman for you, Jack. She's bright, she's funny and she loves you. What more could you ask?"

Jack laughed. "You could see that? That she loves me? I didn't realize it was that obvious."

"Hey, I'm your dad, remember? Dads are supposed to see stuff like that. They also see that you love her back. That's good because it works better that way."

"Will you and Pop come to the wedding? Sam's going to be my best man. We'll be a family again."

"You want another beer?" At Jack's nod Michael went out to the kitchen. "A family?" he called. "Will your mother be there?"

There was no answer but when Michael came back into the living room Jack gave him a long look. "Would that matter?" he asked in a quiet voice.

Michael realized what was going through his son's mind. "No. No, I don't think so. In fact, I'd kind of like to see her again. It's probably been long enough that most of the hurt and anger has been worked through. Mine has, certainly. I hope hers has as well."

Jack accepted his beer. "Would it bother you that she's gotten remarried? He'll be there too."

"Is he a nice guy?"

"We think so. He's not you but, yeah, he's a nice guy."

"Then I'll shake his hand and wish him all the best." He grinned. "And I won't tell him any secrets she hasn't already told him. Okay?"

Jack stood and hugged his father. "Thanks, Dad.

———————

The wedding was beautiful, just as they'd known it would be since Claire had planned it. Claire was beautiful as well, in a dress she had designed and her mother had made. And it nearly burst Michael's heart to see how beautiful both his boys were, standing up straight in their tuxedos and with polished shoes no one had had to tell them to polish. Even Clyde, Joanne's new husband, was handsome and fit right in.

There was a second wedding, a year and a half later. This time it was Sam and Ann, the woman he'd been living with for a couple of years. Sam confided in his father that he and Ann had decided it was finally time to have a child. "She isn't pregnant yet," Sam said, "but I can tell you this: I sure won't miss those condoms."

Michael smiled. "Neither will she, Son, neither will she."

It didn't take long. One year later, to the day, a daughter, Nicole, was born. A year after that, a son, Webster, came along.

"And that's all," Sam said when Michael and George came to see the new grandson.

"Uh oh, back to the condoms, huh?" George said.

"Not on your life," Sam answered with a grin. "We both had our tubes tied."

———————

A few years later two things happened: George turned sixty-five and he became a writer. He'd been doing academic writing all his professional life but academic writing and what he wrote after retirement were two widely different things. His first book was titled *Stud Boy Ranch* and it sold a surprising number of copies. Enough so that the publisher was anxious to bring out his second book, *Locker Room Lovers*.

George's publisher told him that if he was ever in Palm Springs, California, there was a large bookstore there which would love to have him do a book signing. They couldn't pay him to go there but they would certainly buy him dinner if he did.

"So let's go," Michael said when George told him about it. "We've never been there and I understand that it's quite a nice town."

It was a nice town. And friendly, too. The bookstore owners threw a big signing party for George, complete with champagne and little hors d'oeuvres, and a lot of guys came to buy his book and have him sign it. Some even brought his first one and he gladly signed those, too.

They spent a week in Palm Springs and the longer they were there the more they liked it. So much so that when Michael retired the next year they packed up, sold their house and moved there.

At the book signing they had made friends with a handsome, surprisingly hunky real estate guy named Victor. When they decided to move to Palm Springs, they called him and sure enough, he had the perfect place for them: Number 15 Taylor Circle. They moved in on tax day, April 15, 1999.

TAYLOR CIRCLE

The day was cold by Palm Springs standards, perhaps seventy-one degrees. Michael and George, however, didn't think so being as how they had left an early spring snow storm only three days before.

"Oh God, I'm going to love it here," Michael said, hunting through his suitcase, looking for a bathing suit. "It's warm, this house is wonderful and best of all, we have our very own swimming pool." He found what he was looking for and stripped off his jeans. Pulling on his suit he looked at George. "Well, aren't you going to swim with me?"

"I am. But why are you putting on a bathing suit?" He licked his lips. "Afraid the sight of your nakedness will inflame me with passion?"

Michael stopped, the bathing suit around his knees. "What are you talking about?"

George laughed. "Michael, it's our pool. There's a six foot concrete block wall around it. The only people who can see us are in airplanes twenty thousand feet in the air. And no matter how big you might think you are, I guarantee they will not be able to see your dick."

Michael stood still for a moment before he burst out laughing and pushed the suit to his ankles. "You know," he said, looking up at George, "I just didn't think about it. I don't think I've been naked in a pool since I was at boy scout camp when I was eleven." He grinned. "I wonder if I'll get a stiffy like I did then. That probably should have told me something."

Outside the air didn't seem cool at all and the water actually seemed warm. Probably, they thought, because of the solar heating Mike Spraker had put in. They swam for a quarter of an hour and sure enough, Michael got a stiffy. George did too and they ended up on one of the lounges, making love out in the open air and under the warm sun. They knew they were home.

Their first visitor, of course, was Brown, bearing an apple pie Mrs. Brown had baked that morning. "Looks like the neighborhood is kind of filling up with you people," Brown said after the introductions were over. "Got gay guys on either side of me and now you, here at the end of the circle. I'm feelin' kind of old fashioned, what with having a wife and all." He laughed. "Maybe I oughta get me a boyfriend or something."

Neither Michael nor George had any idea what to make of Brown's comments so they just ignored them. "Come on in, Mr. Brown. Can we get you something? Coffee? Or maybe a beer?"

"Oh my, no," Brown said. "Too early for me. Besides I'll probably be having a beer with Bill, my next door neighbor, this afternoon. No, I just wanted to be neighborly and bring you that pie Mrs. Brown made."

Their second visitor was Bill, Brown's next door neighbor. He brought a bottle of wine by way of welcome and, better yet, an invitation to dinner the next night. "I can't stay, guys, but I wanted to welcome you. You'll meet the other guys on the circle at dinner."

It was dinner for six: Wes & Bill, Buzz & Mickey and Michael & George, all recent residents on Taylor Circle. It was a diverse group with Michael & George in their sixty's and retired; Buzz & Mickey in their very early fifty's with Mickey working and Buzz writing a book; Wes & Bill with Wes in his mid twenty's and just starting out as a veterinarian and Bill in his mid forty's and working repairing cars. Nonetheless they quickly found that they liked one another, and conversation never lagged.

"Hey, what's with this Brown character?" George asked the table as they were starting in on their shrimp in aspic with dill sauce.

"Why? What'd he say?" This from Bill.

"Well, he brought us a pie…"

"A very good one, I might add," said Michael. "Apple, my favorite."

"Ours was pecan," Buzz said.

"And ours was apple, too," Bill said, "but go on. What did he say?"

George tasted his wine and found it very good. "He said something about the neighborhood filling up with 'you people', whoever 'you people' are. Said he felt old fashioned having a wife and maybe he should get a boyfriend. Did he mean gays?"

"Yeah," Bill said. "We were the first, they," pointing at Buzz & Mickey, "were second and now you. I guess he's feeling a little outnumbered."

"Yeah, don't worry about it. He's actually a pretty good neighbor, always giving people something or offering to help." Mickey put his fork on his empty plate. "That was one good aspic, Bill."

"And my favorite dill sauce," Wes added. "Thank you for that."

When the plates were cleared and the pasta primavera had been served, Bill said, "Getting back to Brown—and that's what he wants to be called, Brown—he's quite a guy. Has some quaint ideas about male anatomy but otherwise..."

They all laughed and George said, "What the hell does that mean? You talk about dicks with him?"

"Well, not all the time but yeah, the subject has come up once or twice."

"Tell them the story, Bill," Wes said, pouring more wine. "I think it tells you something rather charming about Brown."

"Okay, okay." He had everyone's attention even though Buzz & Mickey had heard the story before. "See, he was over here one day, having a beer... Oh, guys," he said, indicating Michael and George, "be sure to lay in some beer, Heinekens preferably. He likes one occasionally and I don't think Mrs. Brown lets him drink it at home. Anyway, it was hot and I suggested we go for a swim."

"As these guys know," Wes interrupted with a grin, "we don't allow bathing suits in our pool. Well, unless my mother is here."

"So I start taking my pants off," Bill continued, "and Brown asks for a bathing suit. It turns out Mrs. Brown doesn't let him swim naked at home either."

"He knew you're gay, right?" Michael said. "Maybe he was afraid to get naked with... You know."

"No, I asked him that, point blank. So anyway, he shrugs and takes his pants off. Like every other man in Palm Springs, he doesn't wear underwear so there we were, naked together. And he says, looking at my dick, "Ain't fair. You're almost as big as me.'"

"What?" George shook his head and laughed. "What was that all about?"

"Well, it seems that Brown has this theory that in any gathering of men, the blacks will always have the biggest dicks. And I was challenging his theory by having one almost as big as his, the one on the black guy."

Everyone laughed and Buzz said, "He probably hasn't had much experience with naked men. Unlike those of us around this table. You going to tell them the rest or are you going to leave that to Wes?"

"Oh, I'll tell it. From Wes it'd sound like bragging."

"Which it would be," Mickey said, "but never mind. Tell it anyway, Bill, these guys haven't heard it."

"Well, my friend here is quite blessed in the dick department and when Brown got a look at it, it was either change the theory or find new facts. Brown choose to find new facts. He informed Wes that he has a black ancestor. Which explains Wes' endowment and leaves Brown's theory intact. It was a rather elegant solution, I thought."

Everyone around the table nodded in agreement.

"How about Mrs. Brown. What's she like?" George asked.

"We don't see much of her," Mickey said. "I guess Brown pretty much tells her what's going on in the neighborhood. Well, except for swimming naked with us and drinking beer."

"How about the others, like Number 95?"

"That would be the Vartins. You know, I don't think any of us really know them."

"No. You hardly ever see them," said Buzz. "Although I've seen him leaving the house in his car. Black hair, dark complexion, maybe a mustache."

"Oooh, mysterious neighbors," Michael laughed. "Do they howl at night when the moon is full?"

"I don't think so," Buzz said. "They're very quiet people. We never hear them and they seem to always have the drapes closed. Sometimes in the summer, late at night, they go out on the back patio and watch TV but I tell you, the volume's so low I have no idea what they watch."

Mickey looked up. "I think he used to work in the movies, over in L.A. That's what someone at the store told me. He's supposed to be very old school and very private."

"Well, I'm sure we'll run into them sometime," Michael said. "Say our hellos then."

"Don't be too sure," Bill replied. "We've been here over a year and haven't seen them yet."

They adjourned from the table and went to the living room for a last cocktail before ending the evening. Conversation turned to Palm Springs social life and an organization called Prime Timers.

"It's a club for older men and their admirers," Buzz said and then laughed. "I guess that includes everyone here."

"Oh, I don't know," said Mickey. "Bill isn't exactly older, would you say?"

"Yeah, he is," Wes chuckled. "I know because I'm his official admirer."

"Aww, isn't that sweet?" Bill said, giving Wes a quick kiss.

They talked a little more about the club, decided they would all go to one of its mixers sometime and then called it a night.

At home Michael said, "You know? I kind of like those guys, all of them. I think we made a pretty good move, coming here."

George gathered him into his arms kissed him. "We did. I told you a long time ago, we are very, very good together. This just serves as more proof." He pulled away and patted Michael on the ass. "Shall we go to bed and get even more proof?"

Things went along very well for the next few months. All six of the guys did go to a Prime Timers mixer at one of the local gay bars and had a good time. George and Michael joined soon after and the others soon after that.

It was pretty quiet on Taylor Circle until the second Wednesday in June. Buzz and George were standing on the front walk of Buzz's house when a police car pulled up next door at Number 95. One of the officers in the car, a young guy who looked like a rookie to George, went up to the front door and rang the bell. When no one answered the driver got out of the car and came up Buzz's walk.

"Hi, you seen them around lately?" he said, pointing at Number 95.

"Can't say as I have, Officer," Buzz said. "You, George?"

"No. I don't think I've ever seen them. They're pretty private, I guess. Why?"

The officer shook his head. "Nothing much. Their daughter hasn't heard from them in a while and asked us to check on them." He shrugged. "Maybe they've gone to the store or something."

"Doubtful," Buzz said. "Garage door's locked."

The officer looked. "So it is." He yelled at the younger one, "Check the back." While the young officer went to the back gate he asked Buzz and George, "You know anything about them?"

"Almost nothing," Buzz said. "And your guy isn't going to get through that gate. It's locked and braced on the other side. Only way to the back is through the house or the garage."

The officer looked at him oddly. "How the hell do you know that?"

Buzz grinned. "Same guy fixed our gate. Told me about theirs. Some kid evidentially went back there one time and made a mess. They didn't want it to happen again."

"Shit. Now what do we do?" He started towards the car.

"Wait a minute," Buzz said. "I've got an idea. Come on."

The officer called the other one over and they followed Buzz. George trotted along behind.

"I almost forgot," Buzz said, pushing his own gate open. "There's an old gate in the wall back here. Fire Department made them put it in I think although I can't think why. No one else has one."

He led them to the far corner of his backyard and behind a large bougainvillea bush, there was an old, rusted iron gate. Buzz kicked it a few times and when he got it open they found themselves in a small forest of trees and bushes.

"God knows what this is supposed to be," Buzz said, pushing some branches aside. "Looks like a maze of some sort." They finally emerged on the far side of the pool from the house. "Here. Over this way. Back door is there." He pointed.

George went the other way, along the pool and across to the house where he went down a well kept walk. When he came to a sliding glass door he glanced in. "Jesus Christ!" he exclaimed and ran to catch up with the others. "Uh... Officer, I think we've made something of a mistake. I just looked through the bedroom window around there," he said pointing. "They... uh, they're in the bedroom. Fucking."

"Aw shit. I knew something like this would happen," the officer in charge said, slapping his forehead. "Now how am I going to explain this to the Captain? Shit!"

While the officer in charge was worrying about explanations, the young one, for purely prurient reasons, went to have a look. "Uh oh," he said when he looked through the glass door. He turned and hightailed it back to the others. "Don't think it'll be a problem, sir. They ain't fuckin', at least not now. Me? I think they're dead."

The officer threw his cap on the ground, yelled "Shit!" again and said, "Show me."

The three of them followed the young officer around the house where they looked in the glass doors to the bedroom. There, on the bed, was a naked woman with a naked man lying on top of her, legs spread. They could see his balls, hanging down between his legs. There was no motion, not even breathing.

"Okay," said the older officer. "We got to get in there and we got to call the paramedics." He shrugged. "I guess we just break down the door."

"No need," said Buzz. "The door's not locked. You just," he demonstrated, "slide it open." He went to step inside but the officer held him back.

"No can do," the man said. "You guys aren't even supposed to be here and you certainly aren't supposed to see that." He jerked his head toward the figures on the bed. "We'll take it from here and come around later for an official interview. Okay, guys?"

Buzz and George nodded and quietly left, going through the little maze of trees and back into Buzz's back yard where he secured the gate.

At the house they looked at each other and Buzz said, "I don't care if it is only eleven in the morning. I want a drink. You going to join me?"

"Oh, yes," George said. "This definitely calls for a drink."

Buzz fixed vodka-tonics and they took them out on his front porch to watch the action next door. First came the fire truck, siren screaming. It was closely followed by an ambulance and two more police cars. Buzz got on his cell phone and called Mickey to tell him what was happening. Mickey said he'd be right home. Buzz asked him to bring lunch for the four of them.

When Buzz got off the phone he passed it to George who called Michael and told him to come over. By noon the four were having a neighborly lunch of thick, medium-rare hamburgers, skin-on French fries and vodka-tonics while watching the paramedics carefully bring out two sheet covered bundles. About twelve thirty the two original officers came up on the porch, turned down vodka-tonics but accepted iced tea and the leftover French fries.

"Just what we thought," the older officer, who's name turned out to be Tom Avery, said. "I guess sometime last night they just got cozy with each other and Bang off they go."

"But both of them…"

Officer Avery smiled. "Can't tell about the woman of course but him, yeah, just at the end. He'd already... You know. You could smell it in the room."

"Well, I for one say more power to him. When I go, that's the way I want it to happen," George said. "With the orgasm still wracking my body."

"Me, too," said the young officer who's name was Cody Smith. He grinned. "But maybe have it the second or third one."

Officer Avery glared at him. "Don't brag, Cody."

"So what happens now?" Buzz asked.

Officer Avery shrugged. "Nothing much. I talked to the daughter and she'll be coming out Friday to take care of things. You know, claim the bodies, funeral, that sort of stuff. Hey, you ever been inside that place? It's like... well I don't know what it's like but there's these models everywhere. Like miniature houses and buildings? Beautiful, lots of work in them. There was even one of that very house. Had all the furniture in it and everything. You suppose he did that for a living?" He looked around the group.

"Don't know," said Mickey. "I don't think we ever talked to them."

"Well, I'll ask the daughter when she gets here. Meantime, the Captain would appreciate it if you folks wouldn't go talking to the papers or TV or anything. Not until she gets out here. And," he lowered his voice, "please don't talk about what you saw. You know, back there. Okay?"

They agreed, although they spent another half hour speculating about how it had happened.

The next afternoon Buzz was sweeping off his front walk when a new Cadillac pulled up next door, followed closely by a police car. Officer Avery got out of the police car and opened the door of the Cadillac. A handsome, middle aged woman got out and she and the officer went up to the front door of Number 95 where the woman took a key from her purse and opened the door.

A little time passed and just about the time Buzz finished his sweeping and settled down with a glass of iced tea, Officer Avery and the woman came up his walk.

"Excuse me, Mr. Clark," the officer said, "but this is Mrs. Kline, the Vartin's daughter. She would like to meet you."

"And thank you for finding my parents and for your discretion in the matter." She held out her hand, "I'm Nadalia Kline. And you are?"

He shook her hand. "I'm Buzz Clark and we already know each other Mrs. Kline." She cocked her head and he went on. "We met quite a while ago, at a legal convention. We were on a committee together although I can't for the life of me remember what it was all about."

She looked at him for a moment before she smiled in recognition. "Oh, yes. I was just starting out with Hambrick & Holmes then. They sent me to that convention to get me out of their hair for a bit, to figure out what to do with me."

Buzz laughed. "I remember wondering at the time what you were doing at H&H. No offense but they were pretty much a men's club."

She laughed. "Weren't they!"

Buzz waived them into chairs and offered iced tea but Officer Avery declined saying, "I gotta get back to the station and see what trouble Cody is getting into, but thanks anyway."

When Buzz and Nadalia had made themselves comfortable, Buzz asked, "So how long did you survive at H&H?"

She laughed. "Oh, I'm still there. In fact, I'm the Managing Partner now."

"Well I'll be damned. Please," he held out his hand, "let me congratulate you. A woman as Managing Partner at H&H? Man, that is a sea change."

They went on to catch up on each other for a while before Nadalia began stifling yawns. "Please excuse me," she said, but it's been a long day and I think I need some sleep." They made arrangements to meet the next day and see if there was anything Buzz could do to help so Nadalia could get back to New York quickly.

It turned out that Buzz could help a lot and the house was cleaned out within three days. The furniture all went to resale shops in town and the knick-knacks, pictures and Nadalia's father's tools were packed up and stored in Buzz and Mickey's garage until she could figure out what to do with them. Mickey suggested a garage sale.

It turned out that Nadalia's father had been a model maker for several of the Hollywood studios and his work was widely known, both in the film industry and in the art world. She donated all of his exquisite models to the local art museum with the exception of the one of the house itself. That was left for the new owners.

The house went on the market, handled by Victor, the hunky real estate man who had found Buzz and Mickey's house for them. It sold in a week to two men. The men had the same last name but Victor assured anyone who asked that they weren't brothers. They were, in fact, married to each other.

"Oh boy," Mickey laughed when he heard about it, "Brown is really going to be pissed now. Not only will he be the only black, he'll be the only one without a boyfriend. And God help him if one of these guys is hung better than Wes is."

And so, on July 16, 2000, Cliff and Stan Davison moved into Number 95 Taylor Circle.

CHAPTER FOUR

CLIFF & STAN

Cliff and Stan met very early one morning in a bathhouse in Manhattan. They were sitting on a couch in the TV room, drinking coffee, resting from previous encounters.

"You up for that?" Cliff asked, nodding at the TV. One of the men on the TV was bent over the back of a couch, similar to the one Cliff and Stan were sitting on. The two men behind him were team-fucking him, back and forth, in rapid succession.

Stan chuckled. "Not my thing, sorry. I've tried but I never liked doing it, either way." He tugged at his dick. "You?"

Cliff took his balls in his hand and gently squeezed. "Not on your life. There's only one place I want a cock." He turned to Stan and smiled. "I've liked the taste of cock since the very first one I ever sucked."

"Yeah, me too," Stan said. pulling his foreskin up, over the head. His cock was beginning to thicken up.

Cliff stood and moved to stand in front of Stan, blocking his view of the TV. His cock wasn't hard but it was well on the way. "You want a taste of this one?"

Stan looked up at him. "Yeah." He leaned forward and licked across the underside of the head. Cliff sucked in his breath and said, "Oh, man."

Stan moved forward and slowly took the cock into his mouth until the head was in his throat and his nose was rooting around in Cliff's wiry hair. He stayed that way until he finally had to breathe and slipped back a bit, just until it was out of his throat. He took a couple of deep breaths and then went back down on it, all the way.

"Good God, man, you're good at this, aren't you?"

Stan slowly let the cock slide out of his mouth and looked up at Cliff. "So I've been told. You want some more?"

"Oh, yes," Cliff said, grasping him under the arms and pulling him up from the couch and kissing him soundly on the mouth. "Let's go to the playroom where I can get at you, too." He kissed him, pressing their bodies together, their hard cocks pulled up and lying side by side. When they broke he said, "You taste so good. Your mouth I mean, I haven't sampled the other parts."

"It's you you're tasting, your cock. I'll bet you'd love it if you could suck it yourself."

Cliff laughed. "You know? I could when I was twelve. My first time, my very first orgasm was in my own mouth. By fourteen though it was gone. Couldn't reach it any more."

"I never could. Tried hard enough but the best I could do was touch the end with my tongue," Stan said. "But it was okay once my brother let me on his."

They turned into the playroom and laid on the leather covered platform that served as a bed. They twisted into the classic position, face to dick and dick to face. They'd each come a couple of times already that night so neither felt the need to pace himself. They just went at each other, reveling in the twin pleasures of sucking dick and getting your dick sucked. It wasn't long before a couple of other guys joined in, one sharing Cliff's dick with Stan and another sucking greedily on Stan's balls. Pretty soon another crawled over and began to suck on the one sharing Cliff's dick.

Within a half hour there were nearly twenty men on the platform, all connected in one way or another and as soon as one came, another replaced him. The group seemed to take on a life of its own and it lived until something after six in the morning.

Cliff ran into Stan in the showers at six and, without a word, took up a position behind him, reached around and rather handily jerked him off. When Stan came there was light applause from the others in the room, including the cute guy Cliff had aimed him at.

"Man, I didn't think you had any more of that stuff in you. You must have come five times up there," he pointed at the ceiling, indicating the playroom above. "And look, you hit that guy squarely on his dick."

The guy wiped his dick down with his hand and then licked his palm. "Good stuff, too. Want a sample?"

Cliff grinned at him. "No, thanks. I've already had a couple of tastes, directly from the spigot." He turned to Stan. "Can I buy you breakfast? Maybe a bloody Mary to build up some more of that stuff?"

"Hey, that sounds good. And I didn't come five times up there." He hung his head in mock shame. "Only three."

"I can fix that," Cliff said, gently taking Stan in his hand.

Stan laughed. "Later, after I've had my bloody Mary."

They had breakfast at one of the "in" places and then went to Cliff's apartment, undressed and fell into bed with every intention of having sex. They did, too, at about four o'clock when they finally woke up.

When Stan left that evening he carried with him Cliff's card with instructions to call. "Please," Cliff had said. "I really want to do it again."

Stan felt the same way and called on Wednesday. They made a date for Saturday.

It got to be a regular thing, dinner out then back to Cliff's for a glass of wine and anywhere from an hour to the whole night in bed. They liked it best when Stan spent the night because at least then they got a bit of sleep, too. They also went to the baths together sometimes and generally ended up "working over" some guy together. Somehow, sex that involved the two of them together was always more fun.

It took a couple of months before they got around to personal things like how old they were (thirty-six, each of them), where they worked (a surprise: Rightman & Tadish, each of them but in different departments) and where they grew up (Upstate New York for Cliff, Ohio for Stan). They had each had a long term relationship in the past, terminated by the death of the partner for Stan and abandonment for a younger man for Cliff.

"Nine years and he leaves you for a twenty-one-year-old twink? I think I would have killed the twink, I really do," Stan said. "And then I'd have killed him."

Cliff shrugged. "Why? He didn't want me anymore. No, I thought about it but I realized that he'd leave me anyway, if not for one twink then for another. But yours, eleven years and he died? I couldn't have handled that."

"I almost didn't. I thought about… You know, going too. But I couldn't do it. And you know what saved me? Him." He laughed. "No, not from beyond the grave. But when he was in the hospital, at the end, he told me to get out there and live. He said that he'd done all he could to prepare me for life and it was my responsibility to actually use that preparation. If I didn't, it would have been a wasted effort." His voice cracked a little. "I couldn't let it be a wasted effort."

Cliff took him in his arms and held him for a bit. "I'm glad you didn't," he whispered. "Very glad."

They took a vacation and found that they traveled well together. They liked a lot of the same things, men being at the top of the list and it turned out that they especially liked to share their men with each other. Together they never felt crowded, even in a small stateroom. They were both avid sightseers and took every tour they could.

After two years Cliff began to think they should move in together. Stan seemed to be more and more unhappy with his apartment and Cliff didn't particularly like the one he was in either and if they lived together they could afford a better place than either of them had. He was about to mention this to Stan when his boss stepped in and changed the mix.

Mr. Withers, Cliff's boss for the past four years, called him into his office one morning in mid-April and announced that he had been given overall responsibility for the Shareholder Relations Department and he was looking for someone to run it. He'd decided that, if he'd take the job, Cliff was his man.

"Hey, that's great, Mr. Withers, only I didn't know we even had a Shareholder Relations Department."

Mr. Withers laughed. "We don't, Cliff. You're going to create it." His expression turned serious. "It's going to be a big job and it's going to be tough because you'll be wresting some responsibilities away from some other departments and they probably won't like it. However, you will have some help. You'll have a second in command and, within reason, whatever staff you need. This will do several things for you: First, you'll have help and second, you'll have department head status which will mean a hefty raise."

Cliff stood and shook Mr. Withers' hand. "Okay, sir, I'm your man. It sounds like quite a challenge but I'm confident that I can do it with the right help. Now, about that raise?"

Mr. Withers named a figure which quite literally gave Cliff an erection. He had to sit back down so as not to embarrass himself.

They talked about the structure Mr. Withers envisioned for the department and he handed Cliff a thick folder which, he said, outlined the objectives of the department and its mission. He also handed him a list of four names.

"Those are the men you have to choose from for your second in command. I've talked to the managers involved and they'll accept whatever decision you make. I'd suggest that you spend some time with them, take them out to lunch, talk to their bosses and make sure you're compatible with the guy you choose because you're going to be spending a lot of time together. Certainly more time than most men spend with their wives so be sure you can work together. Just do it soon, huh? My instructions are to get it done yesterday."

Cliff looked at the list and grinned. There he was: number two, Stanley Addison. There couldn't be two Stanley Addisons at Rightman & Tadish.

Cliff stood to take his leave but Mr. Withers waived him back into his chair. "Oh, yeah," he said with a grin on his face, "did I mention that this new department will be located in Chicago?"

It turned out that the Board of Directors had decided the firm needed an operational presence in Chicago and this seemed the best way to get it. Mr. Withers wasn't about to move his family to Chicago, not with a son and daughter in high school and a wife who owned a small but very successful gourmet shop. "So it's you," he said. "At least you don't have a wife or kids to deal with. And all the men on that list are single as well." He shrugged. "It's the way it is, Cliff, that's all. Take it or leave it. If you leave it I'll understand but you'll find yourself in charge of finding the two men who will go to Chicago and build the department."

"That's okay, sir. This is going to mess up my life a bit but then, maybe my life needs a little messing up. I still think I can do it, especially with your support and, frankly, guidance." Cliff left Mr. Withers' office with a good feeling about the whole situation.

Cliff spent that evening studying the folder Mr. Withers had given to him and by eleven he thought it actually did make sense. He just hoped Stan would go along with it. Cliff wasn't about to go off to Chicago without the best blow-buddy he'd ever had.

The next morning he visited Stan's boss and asked him about Stan and his work habits. The man was extremely complementary and said Stan was one of his best managers. He also said he was going to miss Stan more than he could say.

"Well then, if you don't mind, I think I'll ask him to have lunch with me so we can get acquainted."

"That's good. You can learn a lot more about a guy over lunch than you can in a conference room or your office. Take all the time you need, too. I might as well get used to not having him around."

Cliff gave him a questioning look.

The man shrugged. "Look, I've worked with him. I know you're going to pick him. He's the best and, from what I've heard, you and Withers want the best."

Cliff took Stan to a place that had just opened and hadn't really caught on yet so there wasn't much of a wait for a table. They had a cocktail before lunch and decided which movie they'd go to on Friday night.

"Okay," Stan said as the hearts of palm and lobster salads were being served. "what's going on here? Why are we eating an expense account lunch, just the two of us? And what were you doing with my boss this morning?"

"Why Stanley, you wouldn't suspect me of having an ulterior motive, would you?"

Stan laughed. "In a word? Yes."

"Well, you're right. This actually is a business lunch." He went on to explain about the Shareholder Relations Department, what they would be doing and, especially, that it was to be in Chicago. He ended with, "By the way, do you have any experience with anything like this? Because I don't."

Stan nodded. "Well, I worked in the Customer Service Department at Lynch & Co. for a while. How different could this be? Oh, and I spent one summer in the Advertising Department at Reynolds." He grinned. "Of course that was when I was nineteen. But I was head of the gopher section. You know, go for this, go for that?"

Cliff laughed. "All in all I'd say you know more about this than I do. You want to do it? We'd be co-managers."

"Probably. Do I get a raise, too?"

Cliff laughed. "You get me and you want a raise, too? Okay, how about fifty percent of what you make now? And a bonus if we pull this thing off?"

"I'm yours."

A week later they were on a plane to Chicago. First class.

Stan agreed that it made good sense for them to live together, even with their salary increases. The real estate man who was handling the office space for their new department suggested they might want to think about buying something rather than renting and, naturally, he had just the place for them.

They talked to some guys in the Finance Department of Rightman & Tadish and, in the end, it did make sense. Especially since, as Vice Presidents of R&T, they were entitled to borrow the money from the company at a very low interest rate.

They looked at a number of places but it was always the first one, the one their real estate man had, that always came up as the better. So they bought it, a two bedroom, three bathroom condo on the forty-sixth floor of a building that overlooked Lake Michigan. It was a magnificent condo with a magnificent view and they were hardly ever there.

For the next six months all they did was work. They slept, but not enough. They ate, usually in the office or on the run. They even had sex once in a while, although there were times when they went more than two weeks without it. It was always a toss-up between sex and sleep and sleep often won out.

But they did it. They put together a department of thirty-five employees offering care and comfort to a shareholder base of over twelve thousand, some of whom held in excess of ten million dollars worth of shares.

But the pace slowed after six months and they found times when they could get away and play. They flew down to Key West and stayed at a resort where nobody, including the desk clerk and the guys who made the beds and cleaned the rooms, wore clothes. They played with the other guys, sometimes separately but mostly together and they played with each other. That weeks' vacation did more to revitalize them than anything else they could have done. Their relationship was taking on shape and character.

Back in Chicago they finally found the time to take their things out of storage in New York and decide what they would keep and what would be sold or sent to the gay thrift stores. They bought some new stuff, too, among other things a new, king sized bed and new desks. They started going out in the evenings again too, mainly to gay restaurants and, of course, gay bars.

One night they wandered into a bar they hadn't been in before, a place called The Prison Yard. Looking around, they quickly concluded that it was very much a leather bar. "You okay with this, Stan?" Cliff asked, watching Stan look around. "I mean, we can go over…"

"No, let's stay here for a while," Stan said. "It's… It's interesting."

"I'll say. Look at that stud over there. In the leather pants? Wouldn't you like to get your hands on that thing he's carrying between his legs?"

"Or my mouth. Jesus, Cliff, look at all these guys. Wouldn't you like to get your mouth on any one of them?"

They ordered drinks and looked at a guy wearing leather chaps, a black silk-looking pouch and no shirt. As their drinks were served the guy made eye contact with Cliff and came over.

"You doing okay?" he asked Cliff.

"Oh, yeah," Cliff said putting out his hand. "Name's Cliff."

The man shook his hand. "Rocky," he said, looking at Stan. "This your boy?"

Cliff nodded.

"Too bad he's taken," Rocky said. "He looks like a good one. Like to have one like him." He looked up at Cliff. "You mind if I touch, see what he's got?"

"Uh… No, I guess not. Go easy though."

Rocky reached out and put his palm on Stan's cheek and then took his thumb and lightly slid it along Stan's mouth. "Nice," he said. "Soft lips, bet they feel good on you." He ran his hand down Stan's chest and across his abdomen, then over Stan's cock. "And a big guy to boot." He looked at Cliff. "Man, you are one lucky son-of-a-bitch." He put his hand on Cliff's shoulder and squeezed. "You ever get tired of him, you just let me know. I'll take him off your hands."

He stepped back and both Cliff and Stan could see that the silk looking pouch was now stretched tight over an obvious erection. Rocky looked down at himself and grinned. "See what your boy does to me? Now I gotta go back to the playroom and get it off again." He saluted Cliff. "See you later, man."

Stan, who hadn't touched his drink during the whole exchange, swallowed about half of it. "My God, what was that all about?"

Cliff reached down and ran his hand over Stan's crotch, then laughed. "He wasn't the only one with a hard-on was he? That little exchange turn you on?"

Stan looked off into the middle distance for a moment. "Yeah, I guess it did. Wow."

"You like being someone's boy?"

Stan didn't answer. Instead he said, "Look at that." He indicated a couple of guys just coming in the door. "What are they…"

It was an older man dressed completely in black leather. Beside him was a wiry man of about twenty-two dressed in cowboy boots, very tight jeans, a Western shirt and a Stetson. He was also wearing a studded leather collar which was secured around his neck by a large padlock. Attached to the collar was a leash which the older man held in his hand.

Cliff shrugged. "I guess the cowboy is his boy and he doesn't want him to run away." He finished his drink. "You want to leave or maybe go back to the playroom or have another drink. Your choice."

Stan looked around. "Another drink."

Cliff signaled the bartender. "Yeah, another drink is a good choice. We're not exactly dressed for the playroom."

"What do you mean?"

"Well, for one thing, we're wearing underwear and nobody wants to screw around with digging for your dick in your underwear. For another, those are hundred dollar jeans you're wearing and they'd probably come out torn, scuffed and filthy. Look at those guys," he said, handing Stan his drink, "cheap sneakers, old, worn jeans and tee shirts. Or like Rocky, sturdy boots, no shirt and nothing but a little pouch to get out of the way."

"I see what you mean," Stan said. "Too bad, too. I'd like to see what the playroom is like."

Cliff laughed. "Yeah, and Rocky's dick. I'm sure you'd like to see what that's like, too."

Stan laughed. "And you wouldn't?"

Cliff tried to look angelic but even in the dim light of the bar couldn't carry it off. "Yes, I guess I would."

They had a couple more drinks and left, both knowing that they'd be back soon.

But not as soon as they might have liked. A week after their visit to The Prison Yard they were summoned to New York.

"Well, well, gentlemen, good to see you," Mr. Withers said when they arrived at the office on Tuesday morning. "Glad you could make it," he added, shaking their hands. A moment later Mr. Withers' secretary came in with a tray of coffee and pastries. The secretary poured the coffee and passed the plate of pastries which turned out to be very, very good and Cliff wished he'd taken two. He noticed that Mr. Withers had taken two and the secretary took the plate with her when she left, presumably for the benefit of the people working in the outer office.

After some small talk about the difference in weather between New York and Chicago, Mr. Withers wiped his hands on a napkin and smiled at them. "I suppose you're wondering why you were brought to New York when you no doubt have things to do in Chicago. Well, the Board has had several meetings about your new department and the way you managed to set it up and get it into operation so quickly. I was called in to their last meeting and told to get you out here to meet with them. You'll note that I was told, not asked."

"Uh oh," Cliff said to no one in particular. "I knew we were in trouble."

Stan nodded. "I had that feeling myself."

Mr. Withers laughed. "No, no men, it's nothing like that. But I don't know what it is either." He looked at his watch. "But we'll know soon. They want us in the boardroom at ten which it almost is." He stood. "Shall we go?"

They went.

The meeting was formal, rapid and a complete surprise to all three of them. First Cliff and Stan were introduced to, and shook hands with, each of the board members. Then the Chairman gave each of them a certificate of appreciation signed by each of the board members. Lastly the Chairman made a little speech in which he said that the board wished to offer them some material thanks but unfortunately Rightman & Tadish was experiencing a serious cash flow problem at the moment which precluded any bonus payments to anyone. Because of this, and because the entire board felt that they needed to do something to recognize Stan and Cliff's accomplishment, the board offered to simply forgive their loan.

The mortgage loan amounted to nearly eight-hundred-thousand dollars and the thought of an eight-hundred-thousand dollar bonus gave Cliff an immediate erection. Stan saw it but he was pretty sure no one else did. Nonetheless he handed Cliff a file folder to hold in front of himself.

When the mortgage forgiveness had been accepted, Stan and Cliff were excused. Mr. Withers, however, was not. "I know this comes as a surprise, Bill, but we hope you will be able to help us figure a way out of our cash flow problem," the chairman said to Mr. Withers.

"Come see me tomorrow morning, guys," Mr. Withers said, waiving them out of the room. "We'll talk then."

On the way to retrieve their briefcases from Mr. Withers' office Stan quietly said, "He's got a private bathroom in there. Would you like me to help you out with," he nodded at Cliff's crotch, "that?"

It didn't take long. Eight-hundred-thousand dollars is a powerful aphrodisiac to a man like Cliff Davis. Afterward they went back to their hotel and did it again, taking their time and doing it right this time.

That evening they went to dinner at a very gay—and very expensive—restaurant. "Why not," Cliff said. "Between us we have an extra four-thousand dollars a month. We can afford it."

On the way back to the hotel a very good looking young man stepped out of a doorway and stopped them. "Either of you got the time?" he asked, looking them up and down, his eyes pausing at their crotches.

"Yeah, sure," Cliff said, pulling his coat sleeve back to look at his watch. "It's eleven-fifteen, on the dot."

"Hey, thanks," the man said. "Can I see that watch?" Cliff held out his wrist but the man said, "No, no. Take it off."

When he said that they both knew something was wrong.

"I don't think so," Cliff said. "Well, good night."

The man pulled a gun out of his jacket pocket. "For me, yeah, it is going to be a good night. For you..." his voice dropped an octave, "just give me your wallets and watches and it won't be as bad as it could be." He waived the gun. "Now give."

Stan fumbled with his watch and dropped it. "Damn," he said under his breath.

"God damn you," the man with the gun shouted. "Now pick that up," he gestured with the gun. "It better not..."

In one smooth motion Stan pivoted and slammed the edge of his open hand down on the man's wrist. The man screamed, a high pitched sound of pure agony. The gun went flying and the man collapsed on the sidewalk. Stan pulled out his handkerchief, reached down and picked up the gun. The man was still screaming and cursing but didn't seem to be able to get up. Later they were told that he thought Stan had had a knife and his hand had been cut off. He was convinced that he was bleeding to death. He even felt the weakness of losing too much blood.

Cliff was on his cell phone but needn't have bothered. The police were there in a matter of seconds. They had just been leaving a nearby coffee shop and had heard the screaming. It took over an hour but things finally did get straightened out although Stan never did get his watch back. The police took it as evidence and somewhere along the line it got lost in the shuffle. Cliff and Stan were sent to their hotel in a police car.

On the way, Stan, bless his heart, leaned forward and asked the driver if he would put on the siren for a couple of blocks. "Since I was a kid

I've wanted to ride in a police car screaming down the street and this may be my only chance. Please?"

The driver looked at him in the mirror like he was crazy but he did it anyway, all the way to the hotel. When they got there, it was Stan with the erection.

In their room Stan hadn't even gotten his tie off before Cliff was on his knees, working Stan's hard dick out of his pants. "God I love this thing," he said quietly before taking it in to the base. Stan put his hands on Cliff's head and gently played with his ears which made Cliff's dick so hard he thought it might break.

After a couple of minutes Stan gently pulled Cliff off his dick and stood him up. "Take your pants off," he said. When Cliff started to remove his tie Stan said, "No, just the pants." He took all of his own clothes off and laid across the bed, his head hanging over the edge. Cliff immediately saw what he wanted and stepped up to him, bending his knees a little so he could push his dick into Stan's mouth. He also took hold of Stan's nipples which had become more and more sensitive over the past couple of years. When he gently twisted them Stan let out a long moan, grabbed Cliff by the ass and pulled him into his mouth until his balls were resting on the bridge of Stan's nose.

They stayed that way for ten or twelve minutes, Cliff working Stan's nipples and Stan tonguing Cliff's dick. When Cliff was right on his edge, holding back as best he could, Stan's dick lifted away from his abdomen, quivered in the air for a moment and then shot out a load of cum which landed squarely on Cliff's tie. Cliff gave up his attempt at control, pulled back slightly and filled Stan's mouth with his own load of cum.

A little later, after a long, hot shower and a halfhearted attempt at cleaning Cliff's tie, they crawled into bed and held each other. "Okay," Cliff said after a while, "where did that chop to the wrist come from?"

Stan chuckled. "Well, when I was a kid, you know, eighteen but a kind of puny eighteen, my dad figured out that I was probably gay or at least was going to be gay. Since I wasn't the biggest kid in town—or the toughest—he decided that I needed some self-defense training. So he sent me to Karate school for a while."

"Well, it obviously took," Cliff said. "Man, you were just great tonight."

Stan laughed. "Which? The Karate chop or the blow job? My Karate instructor taught me both of them."

Cliff pulled back and looked at him. "You could do that at eighteen? Jesus, I'll bet you got an 'A' in both subjects."

"Let's just say I was a serious student and made my teachers proud." He yawned. "Now go to sleep."

Sometime in the night he dreamed about riding in a police car with the siren screaming. It gave him another erection.

The next morning in Mr. Withers office, when Martha, his secretary, passed the plate of pastries, Cliff took three. Mr. Withers told them that, indeed, the cash flow problem had been a surprise to him. "Well," he said, "more like a shock but you get the idea. Anyway, after you left we talked a lot about it but didn't get anywhere." He shook his head and continued in a sharper tone, "How those idiots let it happen I don't know. They run the damn company for God's sake and didn't have a clue this was coming. Sometimes I think..."

He got up and began to pace. "So what I want to do, guys, is tell you pretty much everything I know about it and ask for any ideas you two might have." He laughed. "If you come up with an idea or two, maybe you'll get a bigger condo out of it."

They talked all morning and sent out for sandwiches for lunch. Early in the afternoon Martha came in and whispered something to Mr. Withers. He told her he'd take the call in just a moment. When she left he looked up and said, "You boys in some sort of trouble? It's the police on the phone, wanting to verify that you work for me."

Cliff laughed. "Not us. But the guy who tried to rob us last night might be."

"You... Hang on." He picked up the phone.

When the conversation was over Mr. Withers looked at Stan and said, "You really did that? Broke four bones in that guy's wrist?"

Stan nodded. "I guess. I mean, I knew something broke."

"Yeah," Cliff added, "and the guy was bleeding all over the sidewalk. But he's not..."

Mr. Withers laughed. "No, he's not dead or anything. Going to be in a world of hurt for a few months though. Won't be able to use that hand for a long time. Probably not a good thing when you're in prison."

Cliff shrugged. "Well, he's pretty enough to find someone around who'll protect him." He laughed. "Bubba will get a new girlfriend, that's all."

Mr. Withers gave him a questioning look but let it pass. They talked for another hour and decided that it was all talked out. Cliff and Stan said they'd give it a lot of thought and get back to him in a couple of days. Then they took their leave.

Back in Chicago things were going very well. The department was humming along and the staff seemed happy. Stan came up with an idea for solving the cash flow problem and Cliff helped him flesh it out into an integrated plan. They sent it to Mr. Withers who promised to pass it along to the board.

They also made it back to The Prison Yard one evening, this time dressed for the playroom. They both had a good time but Cliff noticed that Stan was very quiet and always deferred to him when they were there. He also made guys ask Cliff for permission before they played with his cock.

A couple of days later, over a drink after dinner, Cliff said, "You never did answer my question, you know. You like being a boy? I mean, at The Prison Yard?"

Stan looked off into space for a moment and then nodded. "Yeah, I guess I do. Being your boy anyway. It makes me feel… I don't know, kind of protected I guess. Like I don't have to do anything, like make decisions. You do it for me." He laughed. "But don't go getting a Master complex! I may like it when you tell me to suck someone's cock at The Prison Yard but don't tell me what to do when we're at the office."

That last was said in a joking tone but was actually quite serious and Cliff knew it. "Yeah. At the office we're equals. And home too. But at The Prison Yard…"

Stan nodded and then cocked his head. "You like being a Master?"

Cliff nodded. "Yours. When you call me 'sir' it makes me hard."

"Yeah, I noticed that," Stan said. Then, in a very quiet voice he added, "It makes me happy, too."

They left it at that.

A week later Cliff announced that they were going shopping. Stan was surprised when the first stop was the AIDS Crisis Thrift Shop. "We're looking for jeans," Cliff said. "Old ones with worn places and maybe a tear or two. With a button fly. For The Prison Yard."

There were several pair to choose from and they bought four. Cliff was delighted when they came across a rack of vests because most of them were black leather, mostly unlined. They bought four of those, too, a couple with neat little inside pockets. They looked at shoes but nothing particularly appealed to them.

The next stop was another thrift shop, this one for sick children. There they found just the kind of engineer's boots Cliff had in mind. The kind with the silver ring at the side, held in place by leather straps.

The last stop was the most interesting. The shop's name was simply Toys but there was nothing in it that might be suitable for children. They bought cock rings, including one that Cliff picked out for Stan. It was a leather strap that snapped around behind the cock and balls. It featured short, rounded studs on the side that goes next to the skin. "See, Stan? When you're wearing this and some guy comes along and gropes you, all those little studs will dig into you. You'll know you've been groped."

Stan ran his fingers around the ring. "But they won't cut into me, will they?

"No, no. They're blunt and not long enough to do more than poke at you."

Stan thought about it and felt his cock begin to fill out. "Yeah, okay. Let's buy it."

The last thing Cliff bought was a small leather strap with a ring attached to it and a leather leash. Stan didn't have to ask; he knew right away what they were for.

The first time Cliff put the little leather strap with the ring around Stan's ball sack, just above his balls, Stan's cock began to get thick. When he attached the leash to the ring and then threaded it through one of the button holes of his 501's, Stan came up full hard. It showed beautifully in the worn jeans.

When Cliff led Stan into The Prison Yard they created a bit of a stir. Stan was very handsome in his leather vest, no shirt and a leash that was obviously attached to his genitals. There were many admiring eyes.

Before they even made it up to the bar an older man asked if he could buy Cliff a drink. "And one for your boy, too, if he's allowed."

"Thank you," Cliff said. "And yes, he's been a good boy today, he can have one too. Scotch, on ice, no water." He laughed and put his hand familiarly on the older man's shoulder. "I know it's a man's drink but he should be able to handle it. God knows he's handled enough men in his time."

The man laughed but he took a long look at Stan before catching the bartender's eye.

Several men came over to talk or just to look at Stan. Stan for his part spoke only when spoken to, always deferred to Cliff and always did what Cliff told him to do. At one point, at about eleven o'clock, a man who had been watching them for a while came over to them. He had his own boy in tow.

"Hello," he said to Cliff and held out his hand. "Nice boy you have there."

Cliff shook his hand and nodded. "Thanks. Yours is pretty nice, too."

"Thank you. May I touch him? "

"Sure. Can I touch yours?"

"His name is Dieter. Yeah, go ahead, see what he has." The man ran his hand over Stan's stomach. "Nice and tight," he looked at Stan. "Uh, you have a name?"

Stan looked over to where Cliff was touching Dieter's nipples.

"Hey," the man called out. "Your boy needs to know if he can speak, tell me his name."

Cliff looked up and smiled. "It's okay, boy. You may speak, answer his questions."

The man said, "Be careful with Dieter's tits. They can set him off and then he has to lick the cum out of his pants." He paused for a moment and then said, "Or maybe not. It's fun watching him do that, bare-assed licking out the crotch of his pants." He turned back to Stan. "Your name?"

"Cliff's-Boy. Or just Boy. I answer to either but prefer Cliff's-Boy."

"Well, Cliff's-Boy, you any good at sucking cock?" He took Stan's hand and put it on his crotch. "A big cock? Like that one?"

"Yes, sir. If I'm allowed to. My man trained me and he said I learned well."

"You want to suck that one, the one in your hand?"

"If I'm allowed, yes sir."

The man walked over to Cliff and Dieter. "Hey Cliff. That's your name isn't it, Cliff?" Cliff nodded. The man pulled Dieter's zipper down and spread the fly. "Feel those balls in there," he said. "They're big and pretty. Look, how about we take these boys back to the playroom and trade for a little bit. I really would like to get my dick in between your boy's lips. And Dieter here does a pretty good job of that as well. What'd you say?"

Cliff glanced at Stan and caught the little smile at the corners of his mouth. "Sure, sounds like a plan." He went over, took the leash coming out of Stan's fly and lead him to the man and Dieter. "Okay," he said to Stan. "We're going to the playroom now and you're going to suck this man's cock. You're gonna do everything I ever taught you, anything that makes him feel good." He tipped Stan's chin up with his thumb and kissed him lightly on the lips. "Make him feel like you do me and you'll get a little reward when we get home. Okay?"

Stan nodded. "Yes sir. Like I do you."

"Good. Oh, and he can kiss you, too, if he has a mind to. And touch you." He leaned in close to Stan but spoke loudly enough so the man could hear. "And don't go coming in his hand like you did to that guy the other night. A man doesn't always want a handful of boy-cum, understand?"

"Yes, sir."

The man put his hand on the back of Dieter's neck. "You hear that, boy? The same goes for you. All of it." He kissed Dieter, a long kiss and it was obvious that it made Dieter hard. "Make him feel good."

Dieter nodded. "Yes sir."

The playroom was crowded and filled with groans, slaps and sudden intakes of breath, punctuated by "Oh, Jesus" and "Yes!" and "Do it, fucker." Towards the back they found a tall chair, just the right height for a man to sit on while some boy serviced his cock. "Take the chair if you want," the man said to Cliff. "I prefer a boy on his knees." He put his hands on Stan's shoulders and pushed him down. Cliff sat in the chair.

On his knees, Stan carefully unbuttoned the man's jeans, pushed them down and reverently took the man's cock in his hand. It was curved slightly to the right, high average in size, uncut and very hard. He pushed the foreskin back and kissed its head.

"That's it, Boy. Show him your respect," the man said, his fingers tracing Stan's ear.

Next to them, Dieter had gotten Cliff's cock out of his pants and was gently extracting his balls. When Cliff took hold of his nipples again Dieter sucked in his breath. "You like that, don't you boy?"

Dieter looked up at him and nodded. "Yes sir."

"Will they really make you come?"

"Yes sir."

"Well then, we'll have to be careful of them, won't we?" Cliff said. "At least until the end."

"Yes sir." Dieter bent down and slowly took Cliff into his mouth, clear to the base.

Once Stan took the man into his mouth, the man put his hands on either side of Stan's head and held him still. "You don't want to go too fast," he said. "I've been watching you all evening, thinking about what it would feel like to have my cock in your mouth. It's better than I even hoped."

He pulled back and began to slowly fuck Stan's mouth. "You like this, boy? Like a man's dick sliding over your lips, in and out of your mouth?"

Stan looked up at him, never moving from his dick, and let his eyes tell the man how he felt.

"Yeah, I can see it in your eyes. You love this. Well then, let's make it last, huh?" He tightened his grip on Stan's head. "Don't move. You let me do that. You just let your tongue do your part, okay?"

Stan looked up at him again. Then he moved his tongue along the underside of the man's cock.

"Oh, yeah, boy, that's it. But not too quick. Gotta make it last."

Beside them Cliff lifted Dieter's head off his cock. "Give my balls some attention, will you? Let my cock cool down a little." He squeezed Dieter's nipples.

Dieter let out a long groan and arched his back. Then he dropped back down and took Cliff's balls into his mouth which caused Cliff to groan.

"That's it, boy, we're almost there. Almost there." The man was taking long, slow strokes in and out of Stan's mouth. "Slow down," he mumbled to himself. "Go slow. Make it last." He did slow down and his strokes became shorter. Stan was holding his lips tight around the man's cock, forcing it to slide back into its sheath of skin when it was pulled back. Then, when it was pushed into his mouth, his lips peeled the skin back, exposing the sensitive head to Stan's tongue.

Next to them Dieter went back to Cliff's cock, sliding down on it until it was forced into his throat and his nose was buried in Cliff's wiry hair. Both of them were breathing hard.

"Almost there," the man said to Stan. "Oh, God, you are one hell of a cock sucker, aren't you, boy? So... So good." There was a long pause and Stan felt the man's thighs tighten, the muscles bulging, and beginning to quiver. He started to talk, whispering mostly to himself. "We're there, boy. Don't move. Just let it come, let it be and it'll come. It's there. Oh, Jesus, it's there." Tears came to his eyes as his orgasm took him.

It was Cliff's time as well. He felt it, a bubble of pleasure in his gut, expanding out to his head, his feet, his dick. When he was past the point of no return he tightened his grip on Dieter's nipples and twisted. They came together.

When it was well over the man lifted Stan up by the armpits and held him. "Doesn't matter what your man says," the man whispered in Stan's ear. "Some men do like a handful of boy-cum." He undid Stan's pants and took his cock in his hand, gently stroking it. "Could you do that for me, boy? Give me a handful of that beautiful boy-cum?"

Stan nestled his head against the man's chest and said, "Yes sir, I can do that for you."

And he did, almost immediately.

Dieter, without being told, slipped out of his leather pants and began to lick his cum out of the crotch. Cliff had to agree with the man, it was fun watching a bare-assed Dieter lick out his pants.

Back out in the bar the two men shook hands and formally thanked each other. The two boys just passed a smile of understanding between themselves. Then they all called it a night and went home for just one more, private, orgasm.

The next couple of years went along without major difficulties and the New York office seemed happy enough just to leave them alone. They found time to do some traveling and even managed to finish furnishing their condo. They ate out a lot and went to The Prison Yard once in a while, just for diversion. It was a good life.

One Wednesday in June they decided it would be movie night so Cliff stopped at the movie rental shop and picked out a couple of things that looked good. When they got home Stan looked over what Cliff had picked.

"What the hell is this? 1957?" Stan held up one of the movies.

"I'll have you know sir, that is a classic," Cliff said. "Not to be missed." He grinned. "At least that's what the guy at the video store said."

"I don't know. Kim Novak? James Stewart for heaven's sake?"

Cliff took the movie out of his hand. "Yeah, and Barbara Bel Geddes. She's great."

Stan shrugged his shoulders. "If you say so."

And so, nine o'clock found them curled together on the couch, popcorn within easy reach, watching *Vertigo*, an Alfred Hitchcock classic.

When it was over Stan kissed Cliff and said, "Man, that was one hell of a movie. Good choice."

Such a good choice, in fact, that they watched it again, the next night. Lying in bed afterward, Cliff said, "You know, I never knew San Francisco was such a beautiful place."

"Or at least it was in 1957," said Stan. "Remember, this is 1993. God knows what the place is like now." His hand moved out across the bed and found Cliff's dick. "Just like this old thing, it's probably changed a lot."

"Hey," Cliff said, feeling himself begin to harden, "it still works doesn't it? Maybe San Francisco is like that, too. It still works."

Stan laughed, threw the sheet back and took Cliff into his mouth. Fifteen minutes later he had to admit that it still worked.

Cliff was still talking about *Vertigo* at breakfast. "That scene where Kim Novak throws herself into the bay... she was so beautiful in the water. The whole scene was beautiful."

Stan knew what he had to do and he did it while Cliff was tied up in a meeting. He went to their travel agent and arranged for a trip to San Francisco.

San Francisco was beautiful. It was also cold, damp and foggy. When they were taken to their room on the twelfth floor of the Mark Hopkins Hotel they found the view outside their windows was nothing but white fog.

"Yes, sir," the bellboy said, "we get a lot of fog this time of year. But if you go up to the top floor, to the Top of the Mark, you'll probably be above it. That is quite spectacular."

Stan looked him in the eye. "You like to come along? Show us the points of interest?"

The bellboy smiled. "I think I'd like that very much, sir, but they don't allow..."

"Not even after your shift?" Cliff asked. "That doesn't seem very fair."

"No sir, after my shift is okay but I don't get off until Midnight and that's... well, that's kind of late."

Stan smiled. "Not if you stay the night. Then it's just about right."

The bellboy sighed. "Yeah, I guess it would be. But not tonight. I... Well, I could tomorrow, though. Monday's my day off."

"Then tomorrow it is," Stan said. "With breakfast on Monday... Blaine is it? Or is that your last name?"

The boy grinned. "No, first name's Blaine, Blaine Williams."

"Well, Blaine," Cliff said, moving close to him, "we'll see you tomorrow around midnight." Then he leaned in and kissed him. He found Blaine to be very enthusiastic about kissing and it wasn't long before all three of them were sharing the passion.

When Blaine left the room he went directly to the staff men's room, went into an empty cubical and jacked off. He knew that if he didn't he'd be carrying around a hard dick for the rest of his shift.

It was just as well they put it off too, because the time difference caught up with them around nine o'clock and they were asleep by nine-thirty.

The next morning they took the map Cliff had made, the one on which he'd marked all the significant *Vertigo* sites and they started across The City, checking them out. One curious thing they discovered that day was that the folks who lived there all seemed to call San Francisco "The City" and you could hear the capital "T" and "C" when they said it. They found this quite curious but rather charming as well.

Their night with Blaine was one to remember. First of all, he didn't have an inhibition in his body and second, he recovered from an orgasm in a matter of minutes. What Blaine liked best was to be in the middle, sucking Stan while Cliff sucked him or sucking on Cliff while Stan sucked him and all the other possible permutations of three bodies intent on pleasuring themselves and each other.

In the morning they took Blaine to breakfast at a place called Sears which Blaine said was where all the true San Franciscans went. True San Franciscans love good food and this was the place. They all ate too much.

After breakfast Stan observed that the day didn't lend itself to sightseeing because it was cold and the fog was heavier than the day before and asked Blaine what he would suggest.

"If it was me, and I was a tourist here? Well, I think I'd catch the next plane to Palm Springs."

"Palm Springs?" Stan asked, "that's down in southern California, isn't it? Why would you go there?"

"Because it's in the desert," Blaine said. "Had a check-in from there yesterday. He said it was ninety-seven degrees, sunny and dry. Perfect weather for lying around the pool and watching the guys." He looked at his watch. "Sorry, guys, but I gotta get to work. I found out yesterday, one of the guys needs me to sub for him and I really can't turn down the money."

They walked back to the hotel together, all three of them enjoying watching the men on the street. When they got to the hotel Cliff said to Blaine, "If you get a chance this morning come up to the room for a good bye kiss. I think we'll be checking out and going to Palm Springs, right Stan?"

"You read my mind," Stan said. "Guys around the pool is my idea of a good vacation."

It all worked well and by three-thirty that afternoon Cliff and Stan were standing at a rental car counter in Palm Springs International Airport. When they asked the rental guy for a recommendation of a place to stay, he grinned at them and said, "With or without clothes?" He explained that there were a number of nice resorts and many of them were clothing optional which, he said with a grin, made them perhaps more interesting.

They settled on a place called Some Guys which was pretty central to everything and very friendly, both the guests and the owners. It was a good choice and they spent five days baking in the heat—both the heat of Palm Springs and that of the other guests at the resort. When they finally had to go home they vowed to come back. Soon.

———————

One night in the Spring of 1995, they were in bed, idly playing with each other and basking in a warm post-coital bliss. "You know," Cliff said, rolling up on his side, "there's something I guess I've never told you."

Stan leaned up and gave him a quick kiss. "What's that?"

"I love you. Have for a while now."

Stan kissed him again, this time a little less quick. "I know. I love you, too."

Cliff pulled back and looked at him. "How do you know?"

"You. Things you do, like getting hard when I call you 'sir' in that certain way. Like how you always make sure I come whenever we're playing with some guy, even if you don't. Like the way you look at me sometimes, when you think I'm not looking. Things like that."

Cliff sighed and kissed him again. "Yeah. Me, too. I guess I've known you love me since back in New York. How come we never said it, either one of us?"

"'Cause that's the way we are, I suppose. I don't know, maybe it just didn't need to be said."

"Well, it does now. Stanley Addison, I love you."

Stan pulled him down so he was lying across Stan's chest. "Clifford Davis, I love you, too."

Cliff wriggled over Stan until he was straddling his hips. He pulled himself up so he was sitting and took hold of both their cocks in one hand.

"Stan?" he said, slowly moving his hand along their cocks, "would you marry me? I mean, if we could, would you do it?"

Stan nodded and flexed his cock which was fully up and hard. "What do you think?"

"I think I'll do it again, that's what I think."

A half hour later they were in the same position they'd been in before and both were panting just a little. "God we're good together," Cliff said quietly.

"Yeah. We are. And yeah, I would marry you if I could."

It turned out he could. In Amsterdam.

It was a fine trip. They flew over in late June and were married on July Fourth. They picked that date because, as Cliff said, it's easy to remember and there's always fireworks on that day.

When they returned they had their last names legally changed to Davison. Nobody at work said a thing except for some of the gay men and women who got together and gave them a card. Mr. Withers, their boss in New York, merely said, "I've always thought of you two as one person anyway," and left it at that.

Two years after that, eating sandwiches at their desks, Stan looked up at Cliff and said, "Why are we doing this?"

Cliff drank some of his coffee. "Why are we doing what, eating lunch? I guess because we always eat lunch at about this time and besides, I'm hungry."

Stan gestured, taking in the room, "No, silly, this. This job, this aggravation." He held up his lunch, "This lousy sandwich. We don't need it, do we? I mean, do you get off on accurate shareholder lists and letters of comfort to lawyers who have to bill a client for something, anything?"

Cliff put his pencil down and walked over to the couch, closing their door on the way. "Come over here. We need to talk."

Stan went over and sat at the other end of the couch. They tried never to be close enough to touch in the office, for fear that that's exactly what they would do.

"No," Cliff said, patting the cushion next to him, "sit here." When Stan was beside him he put his hand familiarly on his thigh and said, "I think I know what's going on here but I want to hear it from your point of view. Now... what are you trying to say?"

Stan thought for a moment, looking off into space. Then: "I think we should get out of here. God knows we don't need the money anymore and all we're getting out of it is aggravation and an occasional pat on the head from Mr. Withers or the board."

"Okay, but what would we do instead?"

Stan smiled. "Sleep late. Do you even remember the last time we made love on a Wednesday morning? We could go to New York and see shows and sleep late and never go into an office building for anything but to pick up some guy we're going to take to bed."

Cliff put on a look of horror. "You mean… not work?"

Stan suppressed a laugh. "That's exactly what I mean."

"Well, I have to think that over." He looked at the door for a moment and turned back to Stan, "Okay, I thought it over. I can have my desk cleaned out in ten minutes."

It took two months rather than ten minutes, but they did it. They'd groomed several people over the years to take on management responsibilities in New York and Mr. Withers, who was on the verge of retirement himself, was instrumental in getting a couple of them to go back and take over the operation in Chicago.

"So," Stan said, rolling over in bed about six a.m. the first morning of their retirement, "what do we do now?"

"Go back to sleep," Cliff said, yawning. "Or, maybe…" He crawled under the sheet and took Stan's morning erection in his mouth.

"Oh, yeah, that," Stan said. "Let's do that."

Afterward, in the shower together, they decided to go out to breakfast. "You know," Cliff said, "a real breakfast with bloody Marys and eggs Benedict and champagne and everything."

"On a Wednesday morning? We'll never find that on a Wednesday morning."

"You might be surprised," Cliff said. "I've been doing some research and found that there are all kinds of places that have real breakfasts during the week."

It only took four days for them to get tired of "real breakfasts" and one evening less to find that the guys who went to the bars during the week were generally not as much fun as the weekend crowd—and a lot less interesting, both in bed and out.

They did go to New York a couple of times over the next few months but that got old too so they went further East and spent a month in Europe. Finally, one night sitting in El Hombre y el Oso in Seville, sampling the tapas, Cliff looked over at Stan, sighed and said, "Well, what now?"

Stan shrugged his shoulders. "Asia? South America? Just go home? I don't know." He paused and then said, "But I do know I'm bored with this."

Cliff sipped his beer and thought for a long while. Finally he said, "Well, you know, maybe we... Maybe we should go back to work."

"Work? Isn't that why we're here? Because we don't have to work?"

"No, we're here because we didn't think this thing through properly. We were both kind of bored at Rightman & Tadish and mistook it for boredom with working. What I'm getting at is, we need something to do. For us, not for some big, indifferent outfit like Rightman & Tadish."

Stan closed his eyes for a moment, thinking. Then: "What could we do?"

"I don't know but we'll think of something. Now drink up and let's go do what we do best."

It took a couple of weeks...

"Remember Palm Springs?"

Stan nodded. "Yeah, we had fun there. We going for a visit?"

"Well, yeah, I guess."

Stan looked at Cliff sharply. "What are you up to, my man?"

Cliff grinned. "Well, there was an article in the paper about the real estate market in Southern California and how it has taken off. It quoted this real estate guy in Palm Springs who said not only was the market good, it was fun. So I called him up."

Stan laughed. "That is so like you, Cliff, just calling him up out of the blue. Did he hang up on you?"

"No, he was very nice. We talked for a long time and I think we need to go out there and see what it's all about. He said that if we come out he'll let us take him to lunch. How about that?"

"So let's go. How expensive can lunch be? Was there a picture of him?"

"Why? Are you already thinking about taking him to bed?"

Stan laughed. "Well, you never know..."

The trip out to Palm Springs was one of those weird times when everything went exactly as planned. The plane was on time; the connection in Los Angeles was short and easy; their rental car in Palm Springs was ready and exactly what they wanted and the resort was full of handsome, naked men.

When they were settled in their room Cliff called the realtor and arranged to meet him for lunch the next day. "He sounds like a really nice guy," he said when he hung up. "He's also very friendly and seems really interested in helping us."

Stan grinned and said, "Don't look now, Cliff, but either this whole thing is going to turn out to be the biggest disaster we've ever been in or we're on the verge of something fine."

"Huh? Why do you say that?"

"Because everything, really everything, about this venture has gone exactly right so far. That usually means that either a complete disaster or something wonderful is lurking around the next corner."

Cliff laughed. "Well, let's hope for wonderful. You want to see who's up on the sundeck?"

Stan unconsciously tugged on his dick. "Sure, let's go."

There were several guys on the sundeck and every one of them was up. The boys had a fine afternoon.

The next day they met the realtor—whose name was Victor—at a restaurant called The Rock Garden. They immediately took to Victor and he to them so conversation flowed smoothly; it was like they were old friends who hadn't seen each other for a long time.

Over magnificent hamburgers and real, honest-to-God milkshakes they talked about their lives and backgrounds and what they were looking forward to. After an hour and a half Victor looked at his watch and said, "Well, we haven't talked much about real estate but I have an idea. I've got to see a client in about twenty minutes so why don't you guys tag along?" He grinned. "You'll get to see an ace real estate operative in action."

The client turned out to be two men in their early thirty's. They had been together for six years and were looking to buy their first house. Victor took them first to a very with-it condo complex. "You'll like this," he said. "On weekends the pool area is packed with lithe young bodies— occasionally a few of them naked."

He showed the men a one story unit with two good sized bedrooms, each with an attached bath. "You can," he joked, "pretend you just live together to share expenses and have separate bedrooms."

The men looked at each other. "Like when your dad comes to visit," one said to the other, with a little edge to his voice.

"No. I told you. I'll tell him about us. I'm just waiting…"

"Why don't you look around a little," Victor said, "while we go out for a smoke." He ushered Cliff and Stan out to the patio and through a gate.

Outside Cliff looked at Victor and said, "Nice exit."

Victor laughed. "So what do you think?"

"They're not ready to buy a house," Stan said. "They're not going to be together long enough. Dad will see to that."

Victor sighed. "Good observation, Stan. And they shouldn't until they've resolved that issue. This wouldn't be a good place for them anyway. It's obvious that a lot of the owners are gay and they wouldn't be comfortable here."

Just then the two men stepped out of the patio. "You got anything else we can see?" asked one of them.

"Well, yeah, I have one other place you might be interested in. It's on the second floor in a nice complex that doesn't look quite as... well, quite as gay as this one."

They actually went to see two other places, both of which the men liked. As they left the second one they thanked Victor and promised to keep in touch.

"You think they will? Keep in touch?" Stan asked.

Victor grinned. "They might. Clients are a strange and wonderful breed, you know? But don't get me started on clients. You guys want a drink?"

They went to a place called Street Bar and sat on the patio. "You guys seemed to be having fun today," Victor said after their drinks had been ordered.

"Yeah, we did," Cliff said, glancing at Stan who nodded. "Those guys we showed around were interesting and I for one learned a lot about Palm Springs. You really are an ace real estate operative."

Victor laughed. "Comes with the territory. If you don't pay attention you won't make any money and you'll be out of the real estate business fast. But if you do pay attention—both to the market and to clients—you can have a lot of fun."

After a while Victor looked at his watch and said that he had to go and asked if they'd like to spend the day with him the next day. "Full schedule," he said, "you'll get a good picture of what this is all about." They enthusiastically agreed.

Back at the resort, Cliff and Stan sat at the pool and watched the mostly naked men while they talked about the day. They agreed it had been fun and that they felt sorry for the two men looking for a house.

"Thank God neither one of us had to go through hiding like that. I don't think I could have done it," Cliff said. "When I figured out I was gay I just came out and told anyone who wanted to know."

Stan laughed. "I just assumed everyone knew. I mean, my dad knew I was gay even before I did and didn't make any great fuss about it. In fact, I'm not sure I can remember telling anyone. They just knew."

"So what did you think about the real estate business?"

"I thought it was fun," Stan said with a grin. "I mean, I know there must be bad days and disappointments and deals that fall through but everything's like that."

"You've always been good with people and you have a great mind. You never forget anything and I guess that's a lot of what it takes."

"Yeah and you're very organized." He looked at Cliff. "You know, we make a pretty good team, don't we?"

Cliff folded him into his arms and kissed him. "Yeah, we do." He kissed him again, until he had an erection. Then he got up, walked over to a guy who had been watching them and spoke to him quietly.

The man nodded and came over and stood by Stan. "That man over there," he pointed at Cliff, "said you'd like to blow me."

Stan looked over at Cliff who had a large grin on his face and nodded. He then got up, took the man by the hand and led him into a little copse of trees, slid to his knees and took the man's dick slowly into his mouth. The man let out a groan just as Cliff stepped up to stand beside him. Stan spent the next half hour moving from one man to the other, sucking on one while he played with the other's balls and then switching. Cliff and the man were kissing and standing very close together and, at the very end, Stan pulled them together and managed to get both their dicks in his mouth and bring them off at just about the same time.

When both had caught their breath they took care of Stan, the man on his dick and Cliff sucking on his balls.

It was a lovely afternoon for all, including the three men who were watching it happen and jacking each other off.

The next day went well. In fact, by the time they were with the fourth set of clients, Victor did more listening than talking except for the technical stuff and the paperwork. He was very impressed with them and told them so at dinner.

"I shouldn't do this because you guys are going to be formidable competition but if you ever decided to move to Palm Springs I'd be happy to sponsor you with my company. We'd be a sort of sub-company within the firm. Think about it."

He saw a look pass between them and Cliff said, "How long? How long would you be willing to wait for us to get out here?"

Victor shrugged. "However long it takes, I suppose. You serious?"

They both nodded. "Look," Stan said, "we aren't very good at being retired. We need to be doing something, something productive but something that's fun. This real estate thing seems to us to be both."

It turned out that it didn't take all that long. They sold the condo in a week and for a good deal more than they thought it would bring. They sorted through their furniture, got rid of most of it and shipped the rest to California. They spent a couple of weeks taking their friends out to dinner, saying good-bye and inviting them to visit. All in all, four weeks and they were on a plane to Palm Springs.

Victor told them they could stay with him until they could find their own place. He'd also arranged for them to start real estate classes with his firm. By the end of the first week Cliff and Stan were settled into a routine of classes in the morning and working with Victor in the afternoon.

One day Victor asked if they wanted to go with him to list a home. "I've sold a couple of places on that street and they're really quite nice. You should see them," he said as they drove over to a place called Taylor Circle. He knew very well that the house would be perfect for them but wanted them to see that for themselves.

They did, and they bought it, the fourth gay family on Taylor Circle.

They called Bekins, and had a truck deliver what little of their Chicago furniture they'd shipped out and placed in storage so they would at least have a bed and a table and then spent a couple of afternoons shopping.

TAYLOR CIRCLE

Cliff and Stan's first visitor, other than Victor, was, of course, Brown, bearing a peach pie. "Mrs. Brown likes to welcome any new folks with one of her special pies." He laughed. "Of course any of her pies are special."

They invited him in and offered him iced tea or a drink or a beer.

"Well now," he said, "a beer would go mighty good with this hot weather we're having. Must be a hundred degrees out there." He looked around. "You got the swamp cooler going?"

"Swamp cooler? What's that?" Cliff asked, opening beers for them all.

"I guess they're rightly called Evaporative Coolers but everybody refers to them as swamps—'cause they put so much water in the air some parts of the year it feels like you're living in a swamp. Now Mrs. Brown, she won't use one. It's air conditioning or nothing for her."

Cliff laughed. "That's what Stan thought at first, that it would make the air too humid but it doesn't. Just cools it a bit. We'll probably use it all the time."

They went outside by the pool. "You know," Brown said, looking around, "I ain't never been back here. It's kind of pretty with all those trees over there. Kinda like a little forest."

"Yeah, I don't know what the idea was," Stan said, "but we kind of like them." He looked at them and cocked his head. Then he looked at Cliff. "Might be fun," he muttered under his breath.

"You met the other folks on the circle?" Brown asked. "You'll like them. They're all like…" He looked back and forth at them. "You brothers? I saw your names on the mail box but Bill, over there at Number 29 said he didn't think you were."

Stan looked at Cliff and then thought What the hell? He said, "No, not brothers. We're married." So there wouldn't be any doubt he added, "To each other."

Brown grinned. "Then I guess you'll like the other guys on the circle. They're all gay too."

"You're kidding," Cliff said.

"No sir I'm not. Let me see, there's Wesley, he's a… what do you call it? An animal doctor and Bill, his…" he shrugged. "partner, I think he calls him, anyway, he fixes cars down to the Cadillac dealer. They live next door to me and then there's Buzz and Mickey on the other side. Mickey runs that big department store down the other side of town and Buzz is some sort of lawyer only he's writing a book right now."

"Hey, we seem to be in some pretty good company," Stan said. "How about those guys across from us?"

"Oh, that'd be Michael and George. They're retired school teachers. They're quiet but nice when you get to know them. And that's about it 'cept for me and the missus. And you. Where you from? You look too young to be retired."

Cliff nodded. "We lived in Chicago for quite a long time but originally we're from New York. We're in real estate—or will be when we get through school."

"Well how 'bout that," Brown said. "You have to go to school to sell stuff?"

"Well, you do to sell real estate," Cliff said. "We go every morning and then work with Victor, the guy who put us on to this place."

"The guy I saw you with yesterday? That one?"

Cliff nodded. "Yeah, we sort of work for him right now."

"Well, dog-gone-it, he sold a couple of these houses," Brown said, his arm taking in the circle. "Must be a pretty smart guy." He got up and went into the kitchen, rinsed his beer bottle and put it on the sink. "I gotta go now, see what the missus is up to." At the front door he said, "Now don't you worry none about that there pie plate. Mrs. Brown's got a friend who saves 'em for her. Lordy she must have a whole cupboard full. You just toss it when you're through with it." With that, he was gone.

Their next visitor was Bill, from Number 29. Cliff and Stan were just backing out of their driveway when Bill waived them down. "Hi, Guys," he said when Cliff ran the window down. "Quick question. You guys available for dinner Saturday evening? We thought you might like to meet the other guys on the Circle. Dinner seems a good way to do it." He handed them one of the cards Wes had had printed up. "Give us a call if you can't, otherwise we'll see you at six on Saturday. We're over there," he pointed, "at Number 29."

"Hey thanks," Stan said. "We'll be there. What can we bring?"

"You. Your appetite." Bill shrugged. "See you then."

———————

On Saturday night they were just a little late because they'd gotten to playing in the pool and neither one wanted to go before the other had his orgasm. They also took two bottles of wine because Stan didn't like arriving at a dinner empty handed.

"Hi," Wes said when he opened the door. "I'm Wes, Bill's other half and you must be Stan and Cliff. Which is which?"

Cliff pointed at Stan and said, "Stan."

"Then you have to be Cliff. Come on in, the other guys are already here."

In the living room they were introduced to Michael & George, Buzz & Mickey.

"Oh, boy," Buzz said, "this is going to upset Brown, isn't it guys? He's left as the sole straight guy on Taylor Circle." He glanced down at both Cliff and Stan's crotches. "I can hardly wait for the first swim party to see if he retains his crown."

"Well, see who's here," Bill said, coming out of the kitchen. "What can I get you to drink?"

"Martinis?" Cliff said, glancing at Stan. Stan nodded.

"Men after my own heart. Martinis it is. We just happen to have a jug of them ready." He went over to the bar and poured from a glass pitcher packed in ice.

Settled in comfortable chairs with their drinks Stan said, "What's this about Mr. Brown and a crown? Does he really wear one?"

Mickey laughed. "Buzz, that wasn't nice." He turned to Stan and Cliff, "What he's referring to is Brown's quaint notion that black men have bigger dicks than white men which gives him the title of the biggest one on Taylor Circle. If either of you are bigger he's going to have to figure out some way to deny it."

"Yeah," George chimed in. "He decided that Wes here has a black man somewhere in his family background."

"Well, he doesn't have to worry about either one of us, does he Stan?" Cliff said with a smile.

"Well, maybe you," Stan said, throwing Cliff a wide grin.

Cliff's only comment was, "Ha!"

"He sounds like something of a character," Stan said, sipping his martini.

"Yeah, I suppose he is in his own way," Buzz said, "but he's really a good guy. He's always doing stuff for you, giving you things he claims to have bought too many of or fixing things, you know. Just a generally helpful and friendly guy."

"And then there's Mrs. Brown's pies," Michael said. "She evidentially loves to bake and is afraid Brown will get fat so she sends them around to us. Her cakes and cookies are good but best of all are her pies."

"But don't try to get the recipe for anything," Bill broke in. "I asked Brown if I could get her pastry recipe and he said nothing's written down, it's all in her head. All of them, everything she cooks. So, when she's gone, they're gone."

"Doesn't seem fair, somehow," Wes said. "I sure would like Bill to learn to make her double chocolate cookies." He smiled over at Bill. "They're just like the ones we had when we were courting." Bill blushed.

Talk turned to housekeepers with the news that Buzz and Mickey had hired someone to come in every other week and clean the house. "He does a pretty good job," Mickey said, "but then, they all do that for the first month or two. The real test comes at about week six or seven."

"Doesn't matter," Buzz said with a laugh. "What matters is that he works in the nude." He looked around with a grin, "No kidding. First thing he does when he gets there is strip out of his shirt and shorts."

"With you watching intently I imagine," Mickey said with a grin. "Do you get any work at all done on that book when he's there?"

"Of course I do," Buzz said. "But I don't mind admitting that I watch him too. Especially when he's vacuuming. He struts behind the vacuum and swivels his hips so his dick flops back and forth. It's a very intriguing picture."

"And he knows it," Mickey said. "He's just one of those guys who loves to show off and, lucky for him, he has quite a bit to show off."

"Uh oh," George laughed. "Is he a threat to Brown's position as king of the mountain?"

"I don't think so," Buzz said. "But of course never having seen either one of them up ready for action, you really can't tell."

"But he really does a good job?" This from Wes.

"I think so," Mickey said. "The place sure looks clean when he's finished."

Wes turned to Bill. "Maybe we ought to check him out, huh? You've always said you didn't like housecleaning."

"And you've never seen a naked housecleaner, have you, sweetheart?" He laughed. "Sure, we could try him out if you like."

"We'll get some of his cards," Mickey said, "and pass them out to the neighborhood."

"Speaking of passing out, I'm about to pass out from hunger," Bill said. "Why don't we get ourselves to the table."

Dinner was superb. They started with Bill's favorite cold soup, vichyssoise, followed by a cold shrimp salad with Kalamata olives, sweet red onions, bleu cheese and three sizes of shrimp. For dessert he had made an Orange Bavarian Cream.

"Oh man, this is divine," Cliff said when he first tasted it. "It is so creamy and yet kind of tart too. What is it?"

"It's Julia Child's recipe," Bill said. "I only made it. She made it up."

After dessert and coffee Michael began to hide a yawn or two and George said, "I know someone here is going to be up late washing all those dishes so I think maybe it's time we got on home, right?" Everyone agreed.

"Oh, that's all right," Bill said, "I'll just set my naked dishwasher to work and they'll be done in no time."

Wes laughed. "You get your dishwasher naked and the dishes'll get done in the morning. You'll be the one getting done tonight."

Everyone left with a chuckle, knowing it was true.

"That Bill is a lucky guy," Stan said as they crossed the circle with Buzz and Mickey, "having a young partner like that. Have they been together long?"

"About nine or ten years I think," Mickey said.

"What was he, a cradle robber?"

"No, not really. Bill told me Wes was seventeen when they met but he wouldn't go to bed with him until he was eighteen. They've been together ever since. You guys want to come in for a nightcap?"

Cliff caught Stan's eye for a second and passed him a message. Stan nodded and said, "Sure, we'd like that."

They all had gin and tonics and took them out on the patio.

"It is so beautiful here," Buzz said, stretching. "Anyone up for a swim?"

They all were so they stripped out of their clothes, frankly looked each other over and jumped into the pool.

When they got out and dried off, Stan asked, "What's with this Brown guy anyway? Does he really have that big a dick?"

"Yeah," Buzz said, "he does. Big, thick and uncircumcised."

"But you can't really tell about size until you see it hard, right?" Cliff asked.

Buzz nodded. "Yeah, I'd say that's correct," he said softly.

"Maybe, then, Stan here could help us with the little comparison that's been taking place most of the evening. You guys up for that?"

Buzz caught on immediately and nodded. "I think so. If he's any good at it. Okay Mickey?"

Mickey, who was already beginning to grow, nodded. "Sure."

"Oh, he's good at it, aren't you, Stan?" Cliff said.

Stan turned and nodded at him. "Yes, Sir." He was beginning to get hard.

"Then you go over there and show them how good you are at making a cock hard. Do it for me. Okay?" By now Cliff's dick was up to the horizontal.

"Yes, Sir." Stan went and stood directly in front of Buzz. "May I, sir?"

Buzz hadn't played this kind of game before but he had a good idea how it went. "May you do what, boy?"

"May I suck on your cock, sir?"

Mickey suddenly saw this was something that promised to be fun and moved up to stand next to Buzz. "Yes, boy, you may suck his dick but you may not make him come. Not yet."

Buzz looked at Mickey and grinned. He felt like a new chapter opening in his and Mickey's life, at least in their sex life. He put his hands on Stan's shoulders and applied light pressure. "Do it, boy."

Cliff moved to Stan's side, standing directly in front of Mickey. As Stan was sinking to his knees, licking along Buzz's chest, belly, abdomen and, finally, his cock, from head to wiry hair, Cliff leaned in and kissed Mickey, a very long, un-neighborly kiss. When they broke he said quietly, "You, too?"

"Not until tonight." Mickey kissed him again.

"You like it?"

Mickey sighed. "I think so. I don't know. Let's try."

"You gonna be his boy?" He nodded his head towards Buzz.

Mickey nodded. "I've always been his boy."

"He ever loan you out? Like I just loaned Stan to him?"

Buzz, who had been listening, said, "I might. To the right man." He reached out and took Mickey's chin and turned his face towards him. "Okay?"

Mickey nodded and kissed him. "Yes. I'm very horny."

Buzz turned to Cliff and kissed him. "Be careful with him."

Cliff ran his hands over Mickey's chest. When he got to the nipples he rubbed them gently. Mickey sucked in his breath and pushed his chest out.

"Harder?"

"Just a little."

"Just a little, what?"

Mickey looked at him and shook his head. "I don't know…"

"Just a little, *Sir.* You want something you've got to show proper respect when you ask for it." Cliff kissed him, his tongue ridding along Mickey's back teeth.

When they broke: "A little harder, Sir. If you please."

Cliff applied pressure to Mickey's nipples until he sucked his breath in. Then he applied a little more. "Suck on my balls."

Mickey hated to give up Cliff's fingers on his nipples but he did, he sank to his knees and took hold of Cliff's balls. They were bigger than Buzz's, not as easy to get both in his mouth at once but he managed it. Then he let one out and concentrated on just one at a time. Beside him he could see Stan sucking on Buzz's dick, taking the whole thing down his throat. He made it look easy but Mickey knew it wasn't. It was a big dick, especially when it was as hard as it was now.

Stan slowly slid off Buzz's dick, looked over at Mickey and grinned. Then he went back to Buzz's dick, licking along the underside.

"Be careful with that," Mickey whispered. "It's very sensitive and you'll make him come that way. Sometimes pretty fast." Then he went back to Cliff but this time sucked Cliff's dick into his mouth.

Cliff and Buzz were kissing and feeling each other's chests. "Your boy is very good," Cliff said quietly. "I can't take much more of this."

"Yours too," Buzz said. "Maybe we should get them up and take care of them."

"Good idea, Buzz. You mind if I get him off?"

"If I can do yours, Cliff." Buzz reached down and pulled Stan to his feet. "Over there," he said, pointing to one of the padded lounges. "On your back."

Cliff pulled Mickey up as well and pointed him to another lounge. "Time to make you happy, boy."

The two men went down on their "borrowed" boys and the boys were so far up it took no time at all before they were each thrashing around on the lounges, moaning and shooting cum in the men's mouths.

Then the boys took care of the men in a similar display of sexual pleasure.

Later, lying in bed snuggled up against each other, Cliff asked Stan if he'd had a good time that night. Stan took hold of Cliff's hand and laid it on his dick which was quite hard and said, "Yeah."

Next door at Number 78 Buzz asked Mickey the same question and received the identical response: a hard dick in his hand. All four of them knew they would do it again.

———————

A couple of days later, when Bill went out to retrieve the morning paper he saw Brown doing the same thing. "Nice morning, huh Brown?" he called.

Brown looked at him and Bill immediately saw that something was amiss. Bill went over to him and asked what was wrong.

"Oh, nothin'" Brown said. "The Missus isn't feeling well, don't want to get out of bed this morning. I guess I'm just missing my breakfast."

"Well, if that's all, you just go tell the Missus you're going over next door for breakfast. Let her sleep. Women need more sleep than we do, you know?"

Brown immediately brightened up. "Really? Well, thank you. I just hate to miss my breakfast."

"Go tell her and then come on over. The door'll be open."

Bill prepared hotcakes with butter and syrup, bacon, eggs and toast. When Wes came in, his hair still wet from the shower, he said, "Hey, what is this? It isn't Sunday again, is it?"

Bill laughed. "Hardly. We're having a guest for breakfast. Mrs. Brown isn't feeling well so Brown is going to have breakfast with us. I figure him for a pretty hearty eater."

Sure enough he was and Bill had to make an extra batch of hotcakes. But when Brown went home to look in on Mrs. Brown, he was a happy man.

The next day, late in the morning, Cliff noticed Brown pacing up and down his driveway. He went over to see if something was wrong.

"No, no," Brown said. "I gotta take Mrs. Brown to the doctor but she's kind of slow 'bout gettin' dressed. She's finding it hard…"

"Hey, listen," Cliff said, "why don't you let us take you to the doctor. We've got that big, comfortable sedan, you know, to drive clients around in. She'll find it easy to get in and out of. I'll go get it."

"Stan," he called when he got to the front door. "Come on. We gotta take Mrs. Brown to the doctor."

"What's wrong?" Stan asked, tying his shoe. "She have an accident or something?"

"I don't think so but Brown is obviously very worried. I don't think he ought to be driving in his state of mind."

Mrs. Brown, when she got in the car, was very grateful for the ease of entry. She was feeling so weak these past few days and something inside her was telling her things weren't right. She was also thankful for the two young men. She knew Brown was worried and he wasn't the best driver even when he didn't have things on his mind.

At the doctor's office Cliff helped Mrs. Brown up the steps and into the building while Stan guided Brown who was now almost beside himself with worry but trying very hard not to show it.

———

Early that evening, while Stan went out to Wang's of the Desert and got enough Chinese food for eight or nine people, Cliff called the other guys on the circle. "We have a problem," he said. "Come here for Chinese." To a man, everyone was there.

"Here's the situation," Cliff said once everyone had a drink. "We took Mrs. Brown to the doctor today. The diagnosis is cancer. A very fast growing cancer and one which spreads rapidly. The doctor says she has, at most, four weeks but probably less."

The room erupted with comments and questions.

When things quieted down, Cliff went on. "Okay, here's what we have to do. As most of you know, Brown hasn't a clue how a stove works and she's not..." He stopped for a moment to wipe at his eyes.

"She's not going to be cooking anything at all," Stan continued for him. "So we are going to keep them fed, clean and as calm as we can." He looked at a paper in his hand. "Now, Cliff and I probably have the most flexible schedule here so..."

"No, I think we do," broke in Michael. "We're retired and have no real restrictions on our time."

"That's true," Stan said. "Good. Between us we can do a lot of the daytime stuff."

"I can too," said Buzz. "A writer's time is his own."

"Except when it's his editor's," chimed in George. "But we get the idea."

The meeting went on for several hours and when it was over they had a plan and a schedule for getting meals to the Browns and a plan for keeping the house clean and for getting Brown out of the house for a few hours every day. The work was pretty evenly spread around, even among the guys who worked in town during the day.

They didn't tell Brown what they were going to do, they just did it. That way he couldn't argue.

The planning paid off. No one was badly inconvenienced by what they needed to do for the Browns and everyone felt good about doing it. Mrs. Brown's doctor called a local hospice and they sent a nurse to see her on a regular schedule. The nurse brought a lot of literature with her which, when read, turned out to have a great deal of very useful information in it. She also bathed Mrs. Brown, changed her bed and rearranged her medication schedule. She was very impressed with the way Cliff and Stan had organized the men on the circle and gave them some new ideas for getting it all done.

A couple of weeks later, on Friday afternoon Buzz saw Cliff working in the front flower bed at Brown's and went over to him. "Hi, Cliff. Hey, you got some time to talk this afternoon?"

Cliff wiped the sweat off his forehead. "Yeah, matter of fact I'm almost finished here. We can go grab a beer and a swim when I'm done."

"Here," Buzz said, "let me help." He grabbed the hose and watered while Cliff finished the planting.

When they got to Cliff's Buzz said, "Where's Stan?"

"Poor guy, it's his turn to sit with Mrs. Brown. She sleeps, mostly and it's pretty boring. Hard to read, too, because her breathing is getting kind of irregular and keeps your attention."

Cliff got them beers and suggested a swim. Buzz seemed just a little shy when he undressed, turning his back when his shorts came off. Cliff noted it but didn't say anything.

After five or ten minutes in the pool they got out and sat in the shade without drying off. "So what do you want to talk about, Buzz?"

"Well... I mean, the other night... you know, when..."

"Yeah. The other night when we four had our little session. You have questions about what happened? How do you guys feel about it?"

"Well, that's the thing. We liked it. A lot, I guess. But... Well, are you, you know, always the... what?"

"Oh, you want to know if I always play the top?"

"Yeah. Like in fucking, are you always the top and he's always the bottom?"

Cliff took a swallow of his beer. "Yes and no. First of all, we don't fuck." He shrugged his shoulders. "We never have. Neither one of us ever wanted to do it, even when we were kids. That's the "no." The "yes" is that yes, I'm always the man and he's always the boy."

"Well, how did you figure out that's what you wanted to be?"

"Didn't. We just started that way and as far as I know neither of us ever wanted to switch. Are you having second thoughts about which role you want to play?"

Buzz nodded. "Not second thoughts but I just started wondering what it would be like being the boy. I... Well, I liked it when you kissed me, liked it a lot and I began to wonder what it would be like..."

"What it would be like to be the boy. Be the one not in charge." Cliff grinned at him.

Buzz sighed. "Yeah, I guess that's it. And I think Mickey feels the same way although I'm not sure. But..."

Cliff broke in. "You're not sure. Why aren't you sure? You haven't talked about it?"

"Well, no, we haven't. Do you guys? Talk about it?"

"Oh, yeah. Big time. Remember when you asked us if we wanted to come in for a nightcap? I told Stan I was interested if he was and he said we'd like to. But we talked about it first. A brief conversation but a conversation nonetheless. Don't you guys do that?"

Buzz thought for a few moments. "Yeah, I guess we do sometimes. A little."

"Develop it. Learn each other's body language, eye movements, smiles. It saves so many disappointments and downright arguments." Cliff looked at Buzz for a couple of moments, noting the fact that he was developing a hard-on. "I tell you what, why don't you guys come over tomorrow evening and have dinner with us. I'll bet Mickey has some questions too and we'd be happy to tell you our experiences." He reached over and gently took Buzz's hard dick in his hand. "We'll tell you about our rules too, one of which is that we never play with someone unless we're playing with him together." He pumped the dick in his hand a couple of times and let go.

"We have a rule sort of like that, too. But sometimes I just can't keep it down. Sorry."

"No sorry about it. It's pretty and it felt good in my hand. Maybe tomorrow, if everyone is in the mood, I'll get it in my mouth."

"Would you? Even if I'm playing the man?"

"Oh, sure. A man can do a man and he can do a boy, providing he has permission from the boy's man. A boy can also do a man providing he has permission from both the man and his man. Two boys can do whatever they want to each other. At least that's the way it works for us."

Buzz stood, his erection standing out in front of him. "God I'm horny enough to jack-off right now."

Cliff also stood, his erection standing up, close to his belly. "None of our rules say I can't watch you do that. Of course, courtesy demands that I do it as well." He pulled his chair around so it faced Buzz's, sat down and took his dick in hand. Buzz did the same and they spent ten minutes or so seeing which of them could last the longest.

Saturday evening didn't happen the way it was supposed to. Mrs. Brown took a turn for the worst and needed a lot of attention from all of them.

CHAPTER FIVE

BROWN

On Sunday Bill discovered that Mrs. Brown could no longer speak coherently. Brown seemed to understand what she needed but even he couldn't make words of the sounds she uttered. By Monday she didn't even try to speak anymore and in the afternoon she refused her pain medicine. Even when Brown tried she was adamant that she wouldn't have it. She also refused anything to eat including the liquid diet she had seemed to like.

Then, on Tuesday morning, things changed again. Michael was sitting with her, relieving Brown who had gone out on the patio with George to have a cup of coffee. About ten o'clock Mrs. Brown opened her eyes, looked at Michael and said in a strong, clear voice, "May I have another pillow, please?"

Michael slipped one under her head and helped her sit up in the bed a little. When she was settled she asked for a clean nightgown and then asked him to turn his back while she changed. Again settled she asked for the curtains to be opened and then said, "All of you have done so much for both me and my husband, I can't thank you enough but I do want you to know that I do appreciate it all. Thank you." She blew him a kiss and then said, "I would like to see my husband now. Alone."

"Yes ma'am," Michael said and hurried to get Brown.

Brown went into the bedroom and closed the door.

When he came out a half hour later he was standing tall, was clear eyed and carried the trace of a smile. "She thanks you all again and asks to be left alone for ten minutes," he said, gesturing that everyone should clear the hallway. They all went out to the patio and found George had made a fresh pot of coffee.

After a little more than ten minutes Brown gave a sudden start, nearly spilling his coffee. He looked at his watch, bowed his head and quietly said, "She's gone."

When Michael checked, Mrs. Brown was, in fact, gone. Her ravaged body was in the bed but she was not. He called the hospice nurse who came immediately and started the wheels in motion.

That afternoon Brown asked Bill if he and Wes would mind if he stayed in their guest room for a couple of days. Bill said of course, he could stay with them as long as he needed to.

On Friday Buzz and Mickey finally had the promised dinner with Cliff and Stan. Over a cold pasta and salmon salad they got a surprisingly thorough view of role playing and Cliff and Stan's view of the rules of partnership. The rules were pretty much the same as Buzz and Mickey had established over the years for themselves, except, of course, for the role playing part. But those made sense to them as well.

"You know, it's funny," Mickey said, "our rules were pretty rigid at first, I think because I didn't really understand that there is a difference between playing with sex and making love."

Buzz laughed. "Yeah, and playing with sex can be an awful lot of fun as, I think, you've found out."

"I have." Mickey said. "And then there's this, this being a boy once in a while. I don't know what there is about it, but there's something that I find very exciting."

"Probably this," Cliff said, stroking his half hard dick. "Come here, boy, and see if you can make this thing hard for me." He glanced at Buzz and received a wink.

Mickey didn't move for a moment, until Cliff looked at him in a certain way, sending him a message he could neither mistake nor ignore. He slowly walked over to Cliff and looked him squarely in the eye for a long moment before sinking to his knees, taking Cliff's dick in his hand and licking along its underside.

Buzz whistled. "Man, Cliff, that was some powerful look."

Cliff turned to look at Buzz. "No Buzz. He's doing what he's doing because he wants to do it. My look merely told him he could do it." He let out a soft groan. "And he's doing it very well, too."

A bit later, outside by the pool, Cliff said to Stan, "Let's show them what you can do to a man, only you'll do it to Mickey, okay?" Stan nodded and walked up to Mickey, standing about six inches from him.

"Okay, wait," Cliff said. "Buzz, you come over here and stand in front of me exactly like Stan is in front of Mickey. Now, Buzz, you're going to do to me everything Stan will do to Mickey and in exactly the same way he's doing it. Okay?"

Buzz nodded. He looked over at Stan and saw that his dick was already beginning to fill out.

Cliff nodded to Stan and he started by touching Mickey everywhere, very lightly. Buzz did the same to Cliff. It was very exciting at first, especially when Cliff moaned. When Stan licked over Mickey's chest and sucked on his nipples, Buzz did the same to Cliff. He could feel Cliff's dick poking at him.

Stan finally got to Mickey's dick and sucked it in very carefully. Buzz did the same.

At that point Cliff called a halt. "Stand up guys and take a look at each other." When they did, Stan, Mickey and Cliff all had very hard cocks; Buzz's was puffed up but still pointed at the ground.

"Okay, we switch guys," Cliff said. "Buzz, you take Stan and use him as you would any borrowed boy, while I borrow yours. Okay, guys?"

No one said a word but they moved so that they were each in the right place. It didn't take long for the groans and sighs to start. Again, Buzz was watching Cliff and found he was understanding his actions and what he was doing to and with Mickey and he could see how much Mickey was liking it. He spent time making Stan like what he was doing and appreciating what Stan was doing to him. It was a hell of an experience and one he never forgot.

———————

While Cliff, Stan, Buzz and Mickey were playing, Wes and Bill had gone out for dinner and a movie and some time alone. Brown, who was still staying with them, was tired of TV and found that all the magazines in the house were either about animals or cars, none of which really interested him.

Finally, in the den he came across a paperback book called *The Men in the Trees*. It caught his eye because first of all, the cover showed the backsides of five men wandering around naked in a forest. Second of all he recognized the name of the author: George McGuire which was the same name as the George who lived at Number 15 Taylor Circle. It probably wasn't the same man Brown figured but the idea that it might be intrigued him.

When Wes and Bill came home they saw the light under Brown's door so they knocked quietly.

"Come on in," Brown called.

"Hey, Brown, you should have come with us. It was a pretty good movie," Wes said.

"Yeah, even I liked it," Bill said. "It was a nice romantic comedy. This guy here," he hugged Wes's shoulders, "is really growing up. What're you reading that's kept you up so late?"

Brown showed them the cover. "Just something I found in the den. Hope you don't mind."

"Well I'll be damned," Wes said. "That's George's book. You know, George and Michael?" He paused for a moment, covering his surprise at Brown's choice of book. "You liking it?"

Brown looked at the cover and blushed. He was liking it a lot. "Well, yeah, kind of. I mean, it's a good story." He looked up at them and grinned. "And I'm learning a lot of stuff about what you guys do. Interesting." He thought for a moment. "And it's really him, our George? Over to Number 15?"

"Sure is," Bill said. "You should tell him you read it, he'd be pleased. Maybe give you an autographed copy." He turned to Wes. "Weren't you going to take that over to him and get him to sign it?"

"Yeah but I keep forgetting. Maybe now I'll remember." He turned back to Brown. "Okay, guy, we're going to bed." They went to the door and Wes turned back to Brown with a grin. "Don't glue the pages together, now." They closed the door with a laugh. It took Brown just a little longer to get his meaning and when he did, he blushed. He almost had.

"So he's really reading that thing," Bill said when they were in their bedroom. "I'd sure like to know what he's thinking."

Actually Brown wasn't thinking very much. He was reading and slowly moving his hand along his dick, making the pleasure last.

"Well," Wes said with a grin, "I do know what you're thinking." He looked pointedly at Bill's crotch where the fact that he had an erection was quite clear. Wes was thankful again that Bill had given up underwear, except, of course, at work where he didn't want to push any envelopes.

They spent a long time at it, first on their sides, Bill behind Wes, stroking his dick in time with his strokes in Wes's ass. They'd learned to stretch it out quite a lot, taking frequent rests to touch and fondle. Then, when both of them were pretty far up, they quit and Bill gently withdrew. Wes then folded a large pillow in two and covered it with a towel. He kissed Bill and quietly said, "My turn."

Bill bent himself over the pillow, his erection pressed tightly into it. Wes, on his knees behind Bill, slathered Bill's opening and his own dick with silicone lube and then pressed it against Bill. He applied easy pressure as the head of his dick slowly pushed into Bill. It took a minute or so for Bill to open to him completely but when he did Wes was able to slide in easily, all the way in until Bill felt Wes' low hanging balls flop against his own. Wes waited a moment before starting, waited until Bill sighed and pressed back against him.

Wes was gentle, you have to be with a dick the size of his, but he was insistent, too, pushing into Bill hard, rocking him against the pillow. Bill, for his part, tried to open himself on the in-thrusts and close down when Wes pulled back but he quickly lost the coordination and simply gave himself up to the pleasure, letting Wes do as he pleased.

They came together, Bill into the towel and Wes into Bill and they made it last a long time. When their orgasms finally faded they pulled the pillows out from under Bill, Bill lay flat on the bed and Wes laid on top of him, his weight on Bill's back, hips, arms and legs. They stayed that way until sleep overtook them, Wes still inside Bill, pressing him into the bed.

It was a very satisfying night.

———————

A few days later, on Saturday evening, Cliff and Stan had a barbeque to celebrate their first sale of a house. They invited all the folks on Taylor Circle: George & Michael, Wes & Bill, Buzz & Mickey, and Brown, nine in all. They had some very good steaks, grilled corn-on-the-cob, twice baked potatoes and a green salad.

Over drinks Brown approached George and said, "I didn't know you wrote books."

"Well," George laughed, "they aren't exactly great literature, but yeah, I've written a few."

Brown looked a little perplexed but smiled and said, "Maybe not, but they're good stories, fun to read."

"Well, thank you Brown. Have you really read one?"

"Yeah. At Wes and Bill's. I really liked it. It made me want to... to pull-off."

George thought for a moment and then grinned. "That's what it's supposed to do, make you want to, uh, to do that." He hadn't heard that particular term before and he found it charming. "Did you?"

Brown turned that sort of deep mahogany color black men get when they blush.

"Never mind, Brown. It's none of my business."

Brown smiled. "No." He finished his beer and then nodded and grinned. "Yeah, I did. A couple of times." He shrugged. "It was a good book."

George reached out and put his hand on Brown's shoulder. "That's a very nice complement, Brown. Twice. Wow. I tell you what, you come around to my place one of these days and I'll give you your very own copy of the book and I'll sign it for you, too. And maybe a couple more where I still have some extra copies. You might like them, too. You want another beer?"

They walked over to the serving table where the bar was also set up. Brown rooted around in the beer cooler until he found another Heinekens. George added ice to his glass and poured a little more gin over it. As they turned away George said, "See those trees over there? The Little Forest as the guys call it?"

Brown nodded.

"Well, that was the inspiration for that book *The Men in the Trees*. We were sitting out here with Cliff and Stan one evening and Stan said that those trees looked like they'd be a great cruising spot if they were in a park or something. I got to thinking about it and just like that," he snapped his fingers, "*The Men in the Trees*."

Brown cocked his head. "A cruising spot?"

Stan, checking to see if anyone needed a fresh drink, answered the question for George. "Yeah, you know, a place where guys go to find other guys who want to help them get their rocks off. Quick, fun and no strings attached." He looked around. "Hey, anybody who wants a swim, go for it."

Brown was still thinking about the concept of a cruising spot when Buzz and Bill got out of their shorts and jumped into the pool. "Oh, yeah, that's what I want to do," said George, pulling off his tee shirt. "Come on Michael."

The rest of the party followed suit and pretty soon all nine of them were in the pool, swimming around, splashing each other and having a good time. When they got out for dinner, no one bothered to put his clothes back on. They didn't after the party was over, either, they simply said good-night and wandered, naked, across the circle to their own homes. It felt good and anyway, who was to see?

Several of them stayed to help clean up but once the dishwasher was loaded and the bar was put away, there wasn't much to do. They said good night to Cliff and Stan, gathered their clothes in their arms and left.

In the house Cliff and Stan decided to have one last drink in celebration of their first home sale. As Cliff was fixing the drinks he looked around and said, "Hey, what happened to Brown? He was helping with the clean up but he didn't say good night or anything. Did you see him leave, Stan?"

Stan thought for a moment and then chuckled. "You know? I just may know where he is. He and George were talking about... Oh hell, come on. Be very quiet and I think we'll find him."

They went out the kitchen door and around the pool. As they approached the little stand of trees they heard a rustling of branches and the sound of dry leaves crunching under foot. Stan lead them into the trees and before long, there he was, leaning against a tree, arms at his side.

"Hi, guy," Stan said very quietly when they were standing in front of Brown. "You, uh, you want some help with this?" He let his fingers slowly trace along the length of Brown's cock. "Maybe make it feel good?" He pushed the foreskin back just a little and touched that deep V on the underside.

Brown nodded, evidentially not trusting his voice.

Stan leaned in and kissed each of Brown's nipples before slowly dropping to his knees and taking Brown's dick in his hand. It was long, thick and pliable, not yet up. When Stan pushed back the foreskin and kissed the head Brown jerked and let out a very quiet moan.

Cliff stepped up close to Brown, straddling Stan's shoulders. He looked Brown squarely in the eyes for a moment and then reached out to run his hands over Brown's chest, finally stopping with his fingers in Brown's armpits, his thumbs pressing lightly on Brown's nipples. Then, after a long moment he leaned in and kissed Brown, prying his mouth open with his tongue. Brown began to whimper.

Cliff's dick was very hard and he took a moment to rearrange it so it was pulled up along the back of Stan's head, resting in his thick, curly hair. Then his hand went back to Brown's chest. The feel of Stan's hair around his dick was like nothing he'd never felt before and it turned him on greatly.

Brown was mumbling something into Cliff's mouth and Cliff finally understood it to mean that Brown was going to come. He squeezed Stan's shoulders with his thighs but that was about all he could do because he was on the verge of coming himself. The feel of Stan's hair against his dick, and especially his balls, was more than he was going to be able to handle. Especially now, with Brown's tongue filling his mouth and Brown's fingers on his nipples.

When it happened it was a very quiet explosion. Brown whimpered and moaned into Cliffs mouth and Cliff kind of growled, deep down in his throat. They both shivered as though from extreme cold.

They stayed that way for a long time, Stan on his knees with Brown's dick in his mouth and his balls in his hand, Brown nearly paralyzed. Cliff's legs were wide apart on either side of Stan, who had Cliff's cum dripping down the back of his neck. Then Cliff stepped back and allowed Stan to rise, Brown's dick still in his hand.

They looked at each other for a few moments and then Brown, out of the blue, nodded at Stan and said, "What about him?"

Cliff wondered how far this thing was going to go and said, "You want to help him out?"

Brown's voice was very quiet but still strong. "I think we should, after what he did for us. Or at least me."

"Let's take it in the house," Cliff said, "on the bed."

Brown nodded and they went inside.

In the bedroom Cliff wiped down Stan's hair and then arranged him against some pillows, sitting up against the headboard. "Okay, Brown, make him happy. And please, can I…" He reached out and took Brown's dick in his hand.

"That'd be something," Brown said with a sudden grin, "if I can make both of you happy at the same time and get happy myself, too." He crawled between Stan's legs and turned on his side a little, making room for Cliff. He took Stan's dick in his hand and studied it for a few moments before slowly taking it into his mouth. At the same time Cliff took Brown's dick into his mouth and was rewarded with a low growl from Brown.

They spent the next hour bringing each other pleasure, kissing, sucking, licking without regard as to who was who. When it was over they stretched out together, holding each other, and went to sleep.

In the morning, of course, they got to playing again. Cliff and Stan found that Brown loved kissing and had very sensitive nipples. He also liked his balls tugged on. But when he started petting Cliff's ass, Cliff sat up and said, "We don't do that, Brown, either one of us. Sorry, but we just never got into it, even when we were younger. But I tell you, if you want that, want to play around there, you'll find just a whole lot of guys who will help you out, especially with that thing swinging down there in your crotch."

Brown simply nodded and went down on Cliff. He was learning fast. And well.

Stan made pancakes for breakfast and when they were through, Brown thanked them and then kissed each of them. "I gotta go now," he said, "got a lot of stuff to do at the house." He looked at them, back and forth and, in a low voice slowly said, "She said that after her I'd be a different man and I am. I can go home again."

He took his leave and went across the Circle to Wes and Bill's where he found Bill cleaning the kitchen and Wes knotting his tie.

"Thank you," Brown said. "Thank you for giving me a place to stay and all the meals you've cooked for me. I owe you a lot."

"Well, you're very welcome Brown. But we were getting a little concerned about you when you didn't come home last night," Bill said and then laughed. "Not that you're a kid who might get lost or anything but…"

"Oh, I'm sorry. I stayed over to Cliff and Stan's last night. We sorta got to…" He stopped, unsure what to say.

"Good for you," Wes said. "You need to get out more."

"Yeah, well, I'll be gettin' out of your hair today. Gotta go over to the house, get things done. But thank you. You, both of you, you done a lot for me."

When he'd packed his suitcase and gone, Bill looked at Wes and said, "Now what do you suppose that means, spending the night with Cliff and Stan? You think it means… uh, well…"

"It means sex, Bill. S-E-X. You know those guys. They play. And from the looks of Brown's lips, they play hard." He leaned up and gave Bill a kiss. "Gotta go, my man. See you tonight." With that, he was out the door, leaving Bill to contemplate whatever Brown's night with Cliff and Stan might have included.

Later that day a large truck from one of the consignment stores in town parked in front of Number 50 for several hours before a lot of furniture was loaded into it along with twenty-four cartons of miscellaneous goods. The lights burned late in the house and the next day many more boxes left on a truck from one of the charity thrift stores. On the third day an outfit called Industrial Maintenance and Cleaning sent two large trucks and five large men. They were there for seven hours.

Everyone who had seen the trucks wondered what was going on but of course none of them was willing to ask.

Not long after that, different trucks arrived, some from Lawton's Department Store, filling the house with new things.

That same week, over at Number 15, George received a letter from his daughter, Melinda. When he read it his first comment was, "Well, I'll be damned," and his second was, "it took long enough." There was also a card inside, addressed to Michael.

"What'd she say," George said, handing the card to Michael. Michael tore it open, scanned it quickly, chuckled and began to read aloud:

Dear Dr. Williams,

I wish to apologize for my behavior over the past years, especially as pertains to my marriage and my relationship with you and my father. I am so sorry and I hope that, even though you have no reason to, you will forgive me and accept my apology.

I would be very happy if you and my father would accept an invitation to my engagement party. It will be a small, family affair and believe me, I count you as part of my family. Please come, bring my dad with you and meet the man who will be my new husband.

With respect and affection

Melinda

He looked up. "And what did she have to say to you?"

"About the same. The party's going to be at a rather grand hotel." A close look would show his eyes beginning to glisten. "You want to go?"

Michael stood, pulled George out of his chair and pulled him into a tight hug. "Of course I want to go. I'd like to get to know your children, just as you've gotten to know mine. When is it?"

George looked at his invitation. "Next week. Not a lot of time to prepare."

Michael laughed. "What's to prepare? Buy air tickets and go."

"No need for that." He held up some paper. "They're included. First Class.

And they had a very good time. Well, what's not to like about first class air travel and a suite on a high floor of a luxury hotel?

Melinda seemed her old self only more mature and not at all scarred by her marriage to the fundamentalist preacher. She had had no children by him for which she was thankful. Besides, her brother Todd's two boys and a girl were children enough in the family.

Irene, George's former wife, had remarried and her husband, Samuel, may have been a little overweight and balding, but he was President of Doane College. Irene had made it to the President's house at last. And she was now wealthy in her own right as well, her father having died and left all of his money to her. Her parties for her husband were legend at Doane.

Johnnie, Melinda's fiancée, was tall, slender, and at forty very handsome and fit looking. He hugged his father-on-law-to-be with enthusiasm and sincerity and then did the same to Michael. He took them aside while the pre-dinner cocktails were being served and said to them, "Melinda has told me all about you two and, frankly, about the problem she had with you. When I told her my brother is gay and that I still love him like... well, like a brother, she seemed to rethink her position." He grinned. "I believe that it was mostly a case of what will the neighbors think anyway. Well, that and that ridiculous preacher guy she was married to. But don't worry, Dad, I'll keep her on track now."

Dinner was lovely. Foie gras sautéed and served in a sharp apricot sauce, shrimp salad, lobster thermidor, and a chocolate mousse cake. Even the children, who showed commendable manners, ate it up like other kids eat hotdogs. George was impressed, not only with the grandchildren but with his son and his wife who had raised them to be that way.

Later, laying in bed, arms around each other, Michael said, "He seems a pretty good guy but what was all that about the gay brother? Is he snuggling up to his father-in-law's money?"

"Not quite," George said with a laugh. "Michael, just who do you think is paying for this room? Who paid for the first class flight out here? And who selected and paid for that dinner which we'll never forget?"

Michael kissed him and shook his head. "I figured Melinda's mother did. Or You."

George kissed him back. "Not on your life, my love. Johnnie, Melinda's intended paid for it all. No, I hardly think he has designs on our money. However I do have designs, Mikey. On your..." He patted Michael's ass. Michael pushed back against George's hand.

"I don't know how you do this, Mikey, but..." George took Michael's hand and put it on his very hard dick. "After all these years, you still do that to me." He reached for the lube he'd put on the bedside table earlier, just in case. As he was applying a thin coat to himself and to Michael's entrance he kissed him on the back and licked partway down his spine. He placed himself against Michael and Michael pushed back, taking all of him inside in one smooth motion.

It was a very pleasurable night for both of them. So much so that they had to do it again in the morning.

Back home on Taylor Circle, George received another letter. "Who the heck is Kyle Films?" Michael asked, handing it to him. "I'll bet they want to sell you some fuck movies." He laughed. "Might be fun to have a couple of them to watch sometime."

George read the letter. "No such luck, Michael. They don't want me to buy one. They want me to write one. They want me to turn *The Men in the Trees* into a screen play. You think that would make a good movie?"

Michael put his arms around George's neck and hugged him. "Yeah, I think it would. You write so your reader sees the things you're writing about anyway." He let George go and gave him a quick kiss. "Of course, I don't know that you know anything about writing movies but..."

"Doesn't matter," George said, waiving the letter. "They say they'll do the formatting. I just have to write it." He looked pensive for a few moments. "Yeah, I guess I'll at least try it. What the hell?"

A week later, across the Circle at Number 78, Buzz got his own letter. After reading it he put on his shoes, went to their favorite Mexican restaurant and bought dinner, went home, set the table and chilled the Margarita glasses. Then he took a shower and waited for Mickey to come home.

"Hey, what's this," Mickey said when he looked in the dining room.

"It's dinner," Buzz said. "Now go take your shower and don't bother jacking-off in there. I'll do it for you later, okay?"

"For that I'll hurry," Mickey said. He did hurry and was back in under fifteen minutes, dressed only in a tee shirt and a pair of shorts.

"Okay, what's up? Is this discussion time or celebration tine?"

"Celebration," Buzz said, handing him a chilled Margarita. "As of today, right now even, you are married to a published author."

"Oh, Buzz!" Mickey said, putting down his Margarita and taking Buzz into his arms, "that's wonderful. They published it today?"

"Well, not exactly. It was last Friday but I just got the letter today. I should get a bunch of copies of it in another few days. But it's out, it's an actual book with an actual ISBN number and everything."

"This is wonderful, Buzz. I'm so happy, you'd think I'd written the book."

Buzz kissed him. "You did, in a way. Or at least we did. I never could have done it without you and your encouragement and love." He kissed him again. "Now, another Margarita?"

Mickey drank and held out his glass. "Please?"

After the dinner dishes were done they took the last of the Margaritas out to the patio and sipped them, watching the stars and listening to the sounds of the night. Mickey noticed a high table covered with a thick pad and several towels.

"Hey, what's that?" Mickey said. "Something new?"

"Yeah," Buzz said, taking off his tee shirt and shorts. "It's a little idea I got from one of George's books and Brown built it for me. You have to be naked to use it."

Michael kissed him. "You want me naked, you'll get me naked." He slipped his shorts and tee shirt off and put them on a chair. "Now what, Boss?"

"Now you get up on the table and lie on your back." Mickey did so, using a conveniently placed step. Then he stretched out on his back, his head on the pillow carefully placed at the top. When he was settled he said, "Okay, now what?"

"This," Buzz said, dribbling some oil down Mickey's chest and belly. Then he began touching Mickey's body, firmly at first but gradually making his touch lighter and lighter. It wasn't long before Mickey developed an erection. The erection was touched also, and his sensitive scrotum with its balls floating inside.

Eventually Buzz concentrated all of his attention on Mickey's dick and balls, rubbing and stroking him up that mountain of pleasure. Having been together for such a long time Buzz could easily—and accurately—judge just where Mickey was and keep him from going over the top. Twenty minutes of keeping him right on the edge had Mickey begging to be pushed over and, finally, Buzz did just that.

Mickey came with a loud grunt, arching his back and covering his chest with semen. It took a long, long time. Even before his breathing had gotten back to normal Mickey reached down and gently took hold of Buzz, saying, "Now you?"

"No. Now bed. Famous authors need their sleep, you know."

It didn't quite work that way. In bed Mickey's ass was so close and so warm and so smooth to the touch that Buzz couldn't resist it. Over the course of the night he had two more orgasms and Mickey... well, Mickey lost count.

———————

In late August, George and Michael invited Cliff and Stan for dinner. Over cocktails George said, "Guys, we have a little proposition for you. Remember that book I wrote *The Men in the Trees*?"

Stan laughed. "That one you said was inspired by our little grove of trees?"

"The very one. Well, it seems that a film company wants to make a film out of it."

Michael broke in. "George even wrote a very good screen play for them."

"I'm not sure how good it was," George grinned, "but they seemed to like it. Anyway, they want to do the film and here's the kicker, they want to do the opening and closing credits and at least one scene in your back yard. In your grove of trees."

Cliff laughed. "A porn movie? In our back yard?"

"Yeah. What do you think?"

Cliff shrugged and looked at Stan. "Why not," Stan said. Then, to George, "Do they pay?"

"Oh, yes. They pay. And, if you want, the company will throw a party when they film and you can invite anyone you want to come watch. They can even be extras in the film if they want."

"Now that might be something," Cliff said, "Wes and Bill naked in a porn movie." He laughed. "We'll tell them everyone has to be naked, in the movie or not."

Stan nodded. "Sounds like fun to me."

And it was.

They invited everyone on Taylor Circle to come and watch the filming, be part of it if they wanted and have a festive, not to mention pornographic, dinner.

Kyle Films did their part as well, bringing rib eye steaks, pork ribs, hamburgers, and everything that went with them. They invited everyone to participate and a surprising number of the guys did, including Brown.

Brown of course stole the show. Every actor there wanted to play with him. They wanted to act with him, too but playing seemed to be something of a priority for them. And Brown was a natural. It turned out that he could get his dick hard when you told him to and he could come the same way. He was a porn director's delight.

Everyone got to be in the scenes to be used behind the credits and everyone thought it was great fun. Several of them even got hard when fondled and everyone got to touch everyone he wanted to. It was friendly and fun and there was a lot of laughter.

TAYLOR CIRCLE

Three weeks after the filming in Cliff & Stan's stand of trees, everyone on Taylor Circle received a UPS delivery. Each package contained a DVD copy of *The Men in the Trees* and a thank you from Kyle Films. In Brown's package there was also a letter from Kyle Film's lawyer and a contract.

And so Taylor Circle goes on. A couple of the homes have been remodeled now and several of the residents have retired. But they're all still there, even Brown when he isn't over in L.A. making movies, and they're all still friends. It's a good neighborhood in Paradise.

ABOUT THE AUTHOR

Greg Bowden is a native Californian and thus a product of California schools in the 1940's and 50's.For a lot of years Greg was well aware that he had stories he needed to tell but he wouldn't attempt to put them on paper because everyone laughed at his pathetic attempts at spelling. Then came The Greatest Invention of All Time: the spellchecker. (Well, maybe the second greatest; the Stall Shower is right up there with it.) At any rate, once he began to write he couldn't be stopped. Over the years his stories have appeared in magazines, anthologies, on the Internet and, now, in books. For whatever it's worth, Greg is also able to say that some of his stories have been translated into both French and Dutch.

Greg lives and writes in Palm Springs, California, and still can't spell. He lives with John, his partner of thirty-eight years and Winnifred, the most stubborn Wire Hair Fox Terrier in the state, possibly the entire world. All in all he's a very lucky guy.

Bowden

323 Kearny

323 Kearny

F KEARNY

18·1

a novel by
Greg Bowden

A
BONER
BOOK

Brothers
Greg Bowden